IPODS IN ACCRA

Sophia Acheampong is a British-born Ghanaian. She lives and works in North London and studied at Brunel University. Her first book, *Growing Yams in London*, introduced the character of Makeeda. Like Makeeda, she is still learning about her culture.

Praise for *Growing Yams in London*:

'Sweet and funny.'
Mizz

'Acheampong accurately captures the roller-coaster of young teenage emotions ... There is still an urgent need for novels reflecting different cultures within Britain and this is a welcome new voice.'
Books for Keeps

'A complete delight from start to finish.'
Chicklish

Sophia
Acheampong

IPODS

IN

ACCRA

PICCADILLY PRESS • LONDON

*Thanks to Brenda, Anne, Melissa, Vivien and the Piccadilly Press Team,
Mrs Mary Osei, Dr & Mrs Thomas Mensah, Rt Hon Keith Vaz MP,
Mrs M Vaz, Mr K Acheampong, Vowusu, Ms T. Bonsu, Mr & Mrs Addai,
Mr K Adom Fordjour, Dr Asuboah, Ms Emelia Aryee, Mr Yildi Sirer,
Mr & Mrs Kwarteng, Dr Rose Atfield, Dr Daniela Amasanti, Mrs P Ramage,
Ms Angelina Aidoo, Mr and Mrs Appiah-Minka, Ms V Agyemang,
St William of York Church, Stanmore and Harrow Libraries.*

First published in Great Britain in 2009
by Piccadilly Press Ltd,
5 Castle Road, London NW1 8PR
www.piccadillypress.co.uk

Text copyright © Sophia Acheampong, 2009

A catalogue record for this book is available from the British Library.

ISBN: 978 1 84812 017 4 (paperback)

1 3 5 7 9 10 8 6 4 2

Printed in the UK by Bookmarque CPI, Croydon, CR0 4TD
Cover design by Simon Davis
Cover artwork by Catell Ronca

For Mum, Dad and Gerald

*A guide to Ghanaian terms and phrases
can be found at the back of the book.*

Chapter 1

Rude Awakenings

'Go away, Delphy!' I said from beneath my duvet.

My sister had this totally annoying habit of waking me early. She had no consideration for the fact that I had been up till two a.m. revising. Well, midnight – then I had to watch the final episode of *Yana's Guest*, the latest Californian teen drama. Besides, waking me up on a teacher training day was just plain wrong.

'I mean it, Delphy!' I said, nearly blinded by the sunlight she had sent streaming into my room. 'Who told you to open my curtains?'

'I did!' Mum called from downstairs. 'And stop shouting at your sister!'

'You can talk,' I mumbled. Sometimes it was like Mum had a

megaphone attached to her mouth. I peeked out at my sister. She was dressed in her jeans and a blue top she had begged me to lend her two months ago. Her hair was in shoulder-length braids.

'Well, aren't you going to ask me why I —' she began.

'Delphy, you're my sister. You always want to torture me, simply with your presence,' I said, smiling sweetly.

'Fine! When everyone starts asking you why you didn't get your vaccinations, don't blame me!' Delphy said, storming out of my room.

'What? Woaaaaaaaaargh!' I jumped up from the bed but got tangled up in my duvet. I ended up in a heap on the floor.

'Makeeda?' Mum rushed into my room. 'Oh,' she said, laughing, as I made two failed attempts to stand up. I saw Delphy laughing from the top of the stairs.

'Yeah, thanks for helping me up, Mum,' I said.

'Sorry. So has she told you?'

'No.'

'We're going to Ghana!' Mum said, smiling excitedly. 'You, me and Delphy.'

'Ghana?' I yelped. 'This summer? Wait, isn't Dad going?'

'No, with your Uncle Raj leaving, there's no one to look after the garage,' Mum said.

Uncle Raj was Dad's first apprentice – we called everyone of our parents' age 'auntie' and 'uncle' out of respect. His children had all moved to Australia, so he had decided to retire out there with them.

'He booked his ticket last month so he can't stay any longer.'

'Oh.'

'I'm sorry, Makeeda – I know Dad promised to take you around the slave forts next time we went to Ghana.'

'But what about my exams? It's my GCSEs!'

'Yes, I know,' Mum replied. 'You don't think we'd let you miss them, do you?'

Well, for a second, part of me actually did think they'd let me skip them. Oh OK, more like for a split second. My parents were totally into education. They both believed that as long as you can get a good schooling everything else is a bonus, and Delphy and I were expected to go into further education. I'm not sure about the subjects I've chosen – English is a defo, but apart from that I'm still not certain.

Sometimes, I wished I could be as sure of my future as Bharti or Mel. Bharti knew she wanted to be a scientist and discover cures for diseases, and Mel wanted to be a top athlete and businesswoman and she was already attending a special sports academy in Manchester. I hadn't heard from her in ages, but she'd promised to come down for our end-of-year prom in August. I wasn't sure what I wanted to do yet. I hoped it would suddenly hit me like a bolt of lightning but Mum said sometimes it could take over ten years! She said you could be in a job for fifteen years and suddenly realise that you were meant to be doing something else completely. That's life, apparently. I knew that's what had happened to her with teaching, but I'd rather not have to wait so long. And, anyway, how was I supposed to decide on a job in the first place?

'Makeeda? Makeeda?' Mum said.

'Yup?' I said, realising I'd missed most of her conversation.

'You're always daydreaming! Listen, just concentrate on your revision for now – there'll be plenty of time for us to discuss the holiday later.'

'Oh OK,' I said. But of course I was going to think about the holiday. I was looking forward to the chill-out period between actually taking the GCSE exams and getting the results – everyone had been going on about it for ages. Even my old friend and maths tutor Nick said there was something amazing about knowing you had finished school legally and could simply work for the rest of your life if you wanted to. He hadn't been allowed to do that either, but he liked knowing he could – at least in theory.

My phone beeped.

Bharti: *U up yet?*
Me: *Just. U won't believe where I'm gonna b 4 hols!*
Bharti: *W?*
Me: *Ghana!*

Less than two minutes after sending that text, my phone started ringing.

'Makeeda, are you serious?' Bharti asked.

'Yeah. Hold on, how come you've got credit?' I replied.

Bharti was worse than I was for running out of phone credit. We were lucky our parents topped up our phones each month. In my case, it was taken out of my pocket money. Bharti was luckier as there were no deductions from her pocket money, but having a mobile phone meant her landline use was restricted to four non-essential calls a month and five homework calls. I understood why Bharti's parents insisted on this (there was a crazy global phone bill a few years back), but I still felt it was harsh. It wasn't like we could say everything we needed to say in a conversation at school. I mean, why send us to school if we're not meant to concentrate on our lessons? Parents wanted us to learn and still cram in vital conversations, too?

'I ironed my brother's work shirts for two weeks – whilst I was watching *Yana!*' she said proudly.

'What?'

'He got into an argument with Mum, so she refused to do it and I offered at a price. I earned about thirty-five quid!' Bharti laughed.

'Gee, you could give Delphy a run for her money,' I replied.

'Actually it was something Delphy said a while back, about making an offer someone couldn't refuse, that gave me the idea. I knew the nearest place Tejas could get his shirts ironed was charging four quid a shirt and he still had to lug them there and back. So I undercut them. It also helped that I made sure every morning I was up and dressed before him, and had my own pile of neatly ironed and folded clothing right in front of his nose,' Bharti said.

'Why?'

'Well, gotta look efficient, Makeeda. Besides, Tejas is a lazy sod!'

We both laughed.

'Aren't you excited about Ghana?' Bharti asked, after a pause.

'Sort of, it will be great to see Nana and everyone but . . .'

'But what?' Bharti prompted. 'As soon as we finish our exams, you get an excuse to do some serious shopping and it won't come of out of your pocket money!'

'Huh?'

'Makeeda, there is no way any parent wants a family member commenting on a lack of wardrobe, especially when you're coming from England!' Bharti explained.

'Yeah, I suppose . . .' I said.

'You still don't sound excited, Makeeda. This is totally illogical!'

I smiled. It was our catchphrase for whenever something didn't make any sense. We got it from a comment Miss Oki wrote on my sociology essay.

'What about Nelson? Last summer we weren't together, because he was in South America and I went to France. Bharti, we barely saw each other and that was when we were a couple!' I moaned.

'Ohmigod, I guess that's true.'

'Exactly! We spent more time together when we split up!'

'Dark days, Makeeda,' Bharti replied gravely.

Last year Nelson and I had split up a lot. The worst argument was when we split up for three months. What started off as a minor disagreement almost ended up becoming a feud of epic proportions. I refused to speak to him until he apologised and he refused to apologise. It was a nightmare as we'd booked tickets to see this top DJ perform in a one-off gig at the O_2. Somehow Jordan, Stephen and Bharti got us back together before the gig.

'I know we haven't been getting on all that well lately, but I guess I was relying on this summer . . . And how am I going to explain?'

'Just tell him, it's the only way. I mean, it shouldn't be that much of a problem, should it? How long are you going for anyway?'

'I don't know, hold on a minute,' I said, walking into Delphy's room. 'Delphy, how long are we going to Ghana for?'

'Not telling you,' Delphy replied.

'Wanna rethink that?' I said, poking her.

She just poked me back. That was the problem with my little sister – she was growing up way too quickly. Delphy was eleven and almost as strong and tall as me. She could actually wear my clothes now. It was weird and annoying for me having to hunt for my clothes in two wardrobes!

'Delphy, see that pink top over there? I could've sworn I bought it for myself last month . . .'

'Fine. Two to three weeks,' Delphy said with a scowl.

'Thank you,' I said, walking out. 'Did you get that Bharti?'

'Yeah,' Bharti said, laughing. 'You're totally illogical with that girl'.

'Why?' I asked.

'I know you were talking about the pink top you don't like!'

'Yeah,' I said, smirking. 'It didn't even suit me.'

'Anyway, two to three weeks isn't for ever. Nelson should have no problem,' Bharti said.

'You think?'

'Yeah, listen gotta go. You're burning up my credit!'

'Huh! That's rich coming from you, Miss Can Chat, Will Chat!' I replied.

Bharti's laughter nearly deafened me.

'Thanks a lot! I've already got a case of RG to deal with!'

RG was our code for Revision Guilt. It didn't matter how much you had done: it never felt like enough.

'Bye Keeda!'

'Bye B!'

So, Bharti was convinced Nelson would be fine about my holiday, but I wasn't so sure. I knew what he could be like when he didn't get his own way. Moody wasn't enough to describe it. That boy could turn cream sour with his moody ways. I'd given up a long time ago trying to snap him out of it. I texted him.

Me: *W R U? Can U talk?*
Nelson: *Nah, out with my mum. Back at Dad's by 8.*
Me: *OK. I'll call U l8r.*
Nelson: *What, no x?*
Me: *Soz. X*
Nelson: *XXX*

It was funny that he always remembered to do stuff like that. At least I had time to think about what I was going to say, but RG was beginning to weigh on my mind, so, shutting out any thoughts of Nelson and my holiday, I opened up my revision notes.

Chapter 2

A Mathematical Conundrum

I was sitting at the kitchen table, staring at a maths equation that Nick had given me. It was number three in a list of twenty that I had to solve. I was feeling quite proud of myself, as I had managed to write answers to all the other nineteen equations.

Nick had been tutoring me for free for nearly two years, but Dad had finally persuaded him to accept driving and car maintenance lessons as payment – Dad's a mechanic, so it wasn't a stretch. Nick was an old family friend and he always used to tell people we were cousins because our maternal grandmothers came from the same village and are next-door neighbours in Ghana.

I looked up and caught Nick watching me.

He had green eyes, olive skin and brown shoulder-length hair in ringlets that his older brother Paul said made him look like a girl. Their features were courtesy of a Ghanaian mother and a Polish father. Nick was at least six foot tall and didn't seem to be stopping there. He wasn't as skinny as he was last year and he was really happy about that. Apparently he had been getting fed up with being called lanky at school. Mel always said he was a hottie, despite the fact that they bickered their way through primary and secondary school. Now and again I could see what she meant, but most of the time all I saw was an annoying tutor and a special friend.

'What?'

'Have you finished yet?' he asked.

'Nearly.'

'In an exam you can't afford to spend twenty minutes on one equation. You have to just get on with the rest of it and come back to that one after you've checked your answers,' Nick said.

'Actually, that's what I'm doing,' I replied.

'Yeah, suuuuure!' Nick smirked.

'Uh-huh. I'm doing exactly what you taught me to do. So shut up and let me finish the test,' I said and that wiped the smile off his face.

Nick had been giving me a hard time since I'd only got forty per cent on a past paper two months earlier. He was so furious, he practically rammed my entire syllabus down my throat and upped my sessions with him to twice a week! If I didn't have a tutor who was one of my oldest friends and a maths genius, I would have been less stressed. I mean, if Mum and Dad had paid a real tutor, they'd never have given me that kind of attitude!

'Makeeda, I wouldn't be acting so —' Nick began.

'Shh! I'm concentrating,' I said.

'If you think . . .'

'Seriously, I really am concentrating and you're distracting me and prolonging the lesson. I'm sure you have your own revision to do,' I continued. He was in the year above and had exams coming up, too.

'Well, I've done a lot already,' Nick replied.

'Whatever! You know you'd be cramming right now, if it wasn't for this lesson!'

'No, you're wrong,' Nick said, blushing.

'No, I'm not,' I said, returning to my work.

'Yes, you are!' he said.

'No, I'm not!'

'Yes, you are, Makeeda.'

I held up my hand to silence him and began writing the answer to the equation.

'There you go, all done!' I said, handing over my answers. 'FYI, I'm not wrong!'

'Yes, you are!' Nick replied, as he slammed his own book down on the table between us with a huge thud. It startled me. He had a look in his eyes I'd never seen before. It wasn't real anger – it was something else. We just sat there glaring at each other. It was really odd, like there was something in the air – something instinctive but frightening. I'd never felt like that before. Then the phone rang, breaking the spell.

'Delphy, get the phone!' I yelled.

'Makeeda, you're not always right,' Nick said calmly.

'Yeah, I know that, because then I'd be this oracle that everyone worshipped and wouldn't really be human,' I said.

'So what, you think you're human?' Nick laughed.

'Very funny! DELPHINA, GET THE PHONE!' I screamed.

'OK, now you've almost made me deaf, but that still doesn't mean you're right,' Nick said, rubbing his ears.

'So you're telling me you'd rather spend time helping me pass my GCSE maths than doing your own revision?' I asked.

'I . . .'

'Just what I thought,' I said, leaving the room to get the phone. 'Delphina, you are in soo much trouble when Mum and Dad get back!' I yelled at my sister upstairs as I grabbed the receiver. 'Hello? Hello Nana!'

The conversation with my grandmother began really well. She asked me if I was excited about going to Ghana and I vaguely said yes, but then she rattled off a whole load of really boring stuff about what I'd be able to do when I got there. All I kept thinking was I'd rather be in my maths lesson with Nick, which was totally illogical! I mean, it's a maths lesson with a stricter tutor than the one being paid to teach me in school. The phone line started crackling really badly and I could only make out every few words. In the end, I got fed up of just saying yes and told her I had to go. I returned to the dining room to find my revision stuff but no Nick. I was a bit annoyed, but then I saw he'd left my test results and I'd only got two wrong! I packed up my things and my phone beeped.

Nick: *Soz had 2 go.*

Me: *Back 2 revision, eh?*

Nick: *Shut up!*

Me: *I know U 2 well :)*

Nick: *Well done on test. Now do pg 20, 50 and 61.*

Me: *Gr8 – u want me 2 do all that on top of my revision and coursework?*

Nick: *NO MERCY!*

At nine p.m., I switched on my PC to find Nelson waiting on IM.

Tunespinner: *Hey! What's up?*

Diva: *Just usual revision nightmare.*

Tunespinner: *I know what you mean. I haven't done as much as I wanted to today, because I was out with my mum. At least I can catch up tomorrow. I still reckon I'd revise a lot more if you were around.*

Diva: *LOL! I don't. We'd both fail.*

Tunespinner: *Yeah, but we'd have a lot of fun. ;)*

To be honest, I knew different. We used to have such a great time, but it wasn't the same any more. It was as if we needed other people around to enjoy each other's company. That couldn't be right, could it? Part of me wondered if I was the only one who felt this way.

Tunespinner: *So when am I going to see you?*

Diva: Umm . . . exams, revision, coursework, etc.
                 Ring any bells?

Tunespinner: Yeah, of course, but you're my girlfriend, so it
                 would be nice 2 see you for more than half an
                 hour a week! I hate being squeezed in
                 between your lessons with Nick.

Diva: Shut up. It's not that bad!

Tunespinner: Yes it is. At least we can hang out all summer.
                 We can see each other every day then.

Diva: I can't.

Tunespinner: What do you mean you can't?

Diva: I won't be here.

Tunespinner: What? Makeeda, I wanted us to go to Alton
                 Towers, Chessington, Thorpe Park, Legoland,
                 even Margate!

Diva: Oh.

I felt awful, but I was also really surprised. Considering the
way we were with each other, this felt like a huge effort. A
little too huge, as far as I was concerned.

Tunespinner: Seriously? I even told Jordan and Stephen, and
                 I was gonna ask Bharti and Mel. Where R U
                 going?

I knew it! I knew he wouldn't arrange something for just the
two of us.

Diva: I'm sorry I'm going to Ghana.
Tunespinner: Ghana? 4 how long?
Diva: Maybe 2–3 weeks.

For nearly three minutes Nelson stopped typing. I thought the connection had dropped.

Diva: Nelson? R U still there?
Tunespinner: Yeah.
Diva: I'm sorry.
Tunespinner: How long have u known?
Diva: I only found out today.
Tunespinner: I wish we could go to all those places together.
               This was meant to be our summer, Makeeda.

I hated to admit it to myself, but I wasn't sure I shared that feeling any longer. I'd begun to think that it would be like all those other times when we barely spent any time alone together. I knew that this wasn't the way I should be feeling about Nelson. I was beginning to feel like a fake girlfriend, in a fake relationship with a boyfriend who was being just as artificial.

Diva: I am so sorry, Nelson
Tunespinner: Me too, Makeeda. Me too.
<Tunespinner: logged off>
<Diva: logged off>

Chapter 3

Questions and Long Distance Answers

I was walking to Aunt Grace's place from the library in Hendon to meet Mum and Delphy. None of my friends understood why I went all the way to Hendon to study but if I revised in any of my local libraries in Harrow, I wouldn't get anything done. I'd keep bumping into people from nursery, primary and secondary school as well as Nelson's mates.

Bharti: *OMG U R soo right. U can't revise in a library in Harrow or Barnet. Everyone knows us! I saw everyone – Pooja, Julia, Laura, Jordan! I mean, Jordan in a library?!*

Me: *LOL! If u saw Jordan, u were defo in the wrong place 2 revise. That boy never stops talking.*

Bharti: *Tell me about it. I now have a serious case of RG, plus I'm at least 4 hours behind in my revision! Off 2 C Meena – she said she cld get me into her uni library and put me up 4 the nite like a real student!! :)*

Me: *Lucky cow!!*

Bharti: *MOOOOOO!! L8r.*

I continued walking when I got another text.

Delphina: *OMG! WOT HAVE U DONE?*

Me: *Use capital letters like that again and I'll whoop ya ass! What are you talking about?*

Ever since my parents had caved in and bought Delphina a mobile phone, I'd got way too many texts from her. I'm not saying it didn't help when you get told to avoid Dad because he'd had a nasty customer who kept calling his mobile, or Mum when she had loads of homework to mark, but that was just Delphy's sisterly duties as far as I was concerned. It was this cryptic rubbish that really annoyed me. I always had to worm it out of her why I was in trouble.

Delphina: *Your conversation with Grma?? W R U?*

Me: *Not sure wot u're talkn about. B there in 5.*

I had no idea what Delphina meant, but I wasn't too concerned.

My conversation with my grandmother had been barely twenty minutes long. How bad could it be?

I walked up the stairs to Aunt Grace's flat. It had two bedrooms, and Afua was living in one of them. Afua was one of those girls who knew everything about Ghanaian culture; she could speak Twi and was so full of herself that I used to hate being around her. It took my writing an essay on Queen Yaa-Asantewaa for my coursework to make her realise that she wasn't the only one interested in our culture. We sort of made up when some old guy had tried to say that our generation had no interest in Ghanaian culture. Since then, and also since discovering that the reason I saw her at every family function was because she was my cousin, we'd become a lot nicer to each other. Afua was living with Aunt Grace because her parents had decided to move to Germany and she, like me, had to complete her GCSEs.

The door opened and I was immediately pounced on by Delphina, who was grinning wildly.

It was Saturday and, unlike me, she had just been lounging around watching heaps of TV, chatting to her mates and generally enjoying the weekend, instead of spending six hours in a library revising. I was exhausted, my dress sense had disappeared and we were only in April! I was concerned about what I'd look like in July.

'Where is everyone?' I asked.

'They've gone to the shops.'

'Oh,' I said, dumping my bag and shoes by the front door. I plopped myself down in front of the TV and

Delphina suddenly appeared next to me.

'What? Stop sitting so close!' I said, pushing her away.

'Well, aren't you going to ask me?'

'Delphina, I know I'm not in trouble so whatever goss you think you have, you don't!' I said, turning up the volume on the television.

'But, Makeeda!'

I held up my hand in her face.

'Makeeda . . .' She began again but was interrupted by the front door being opened.

'Aren't you coming to help us?' Aunt Grace's voice boomed across the small flat. It wasn't really a question; it was more like a command.

'Yes, Auntie,' Delphina and I chorused and we raced to prise the bags from her fingers.

As I began unpacking the shopping, Afua joined me in the kitchen. She was petite, had huge eyes and was never out of fashion. Her hair was in long micro braids, while mine were chunky as I wanted to relax my hair this summer and the thought of spending hours having to undo micro braids was too much. She stared at me with those oversized eyes of hers, for what felt like ages.

'Are you all right?' I asked.

'I'm wondering if you are actually.'

'What? I'm not the one staring at someone like they've grown an extra head!'

'Well, right now, you may as well have.'

'Makeeda!' Mum said, kissing me as she came in with more

bags of shopping. 'Your grandmother told me this afternoon –
I can't believe it!'

I was now starting to panic. Why was everyone behaving
weirdly? First Delphy, then Afua and now Mum. It was like
I'd missed a seriously huge meeting about myself, which is
totally illogical. I had to work out what it was that Nana had
said to me yesterday. All I could remember was the bad phone
line and a whole load of yeses from me.

'Me neither,' Afua said, giving me a weird look. Mum
hadn't heard the sheer scepticism in her voice, but I had and I
was worried.

'Come in here, Makeeda, Afua can finish unpacking!' Aunt
Grace interrupted. She had just got changed into her green and
yellow tie-dye house dress.

As Aunt Grace and Mum sat down with me, the sinking
feeling grew in the pit of my stomach.

I tried desperately to think of what I might have done, but
nothing was coming to mind.

'Are you sure you want to do it?' Aunt Grace asked.

'Do what?'

'The puberty ceremony!' Aunt Grace laughed.

The puberty whaaaaaaaaaaaaaaaaaaaaaaaaaaaaaaaaaaaaaaaaaaaaat? I
didn't remember agreeing to that. I didn't even know what one
was! Oh maaan, it probably had something to do with periods
and stuff. It was weird enough that Dad knew that my periods
had started, let alone the whole world! How had I agreed to a
ceremony? When had I? Why had I agreed to do this?

They must have noticed the shock on my face because

Mum looked concerned.

'Hey, it's OK – it's nothing to be worried about. It's a really unique experience. I could only manage to stuff an egg in your mouth, but this is the real deal.'

I suddenly remembered that, on the day I got my period, Mum had stuffed a boiled egg in my mouth at breakfast and just said, don't bite it, swallow it whole. It was a total shock – we didn't usually do traditional stuff like that in our house. Doing the puberty ceremony would be a hundred times worse. I mean it had to be, didn't it?

I spent the rest of the evening avoiding Afua and Delphina as they both had questions I couldn't answer. It was the first time Mum and Aunt Grace had ever seen me spend an entire hour helping them cook. Somehow I managed to survive four hours at Aunt Grace's without talking about the puberty ceremony again. I knew I'd cope as long as I wasn't left alone with Afua – she'd tell me exactly what I was in for, and I'd decided to live in blissful ignorance for as long as possible. Luckily, she left after dinner to spend the night at her cousin's. So that left Delphy, who was a lot simpler to deal with as there was the threat of exposing her unknown misdemeanour.

My little sister wasn't exactly a normal little girl – I mean, she had this weird, entrepreneurial ability. This meant that she was always buying and selling stuff at a profit. As she'd got older, her deals got bigger and last year she and her best friend Daniel had got caught undercutting her school's tuck shop.

Mum and Dad had made her promise not to get involved in any business arrangements until she got into secondary school. I basically had evidence that she'd disobeyed them. A few months ago, she and her 'business partner' Daniel had sold fashionable bags from New York to girls in my school. She'd told me that it didn't count, as Daniel had actually purchased the items whilst he was on holiday and she was just helping him out by arranging to sell them. But it was great – all I had to say was 'Manhattan' and she left me alone.

By the time we got home, I was completely exhausted, but as much as I tried I couldn't fall asleep as easily as I wanted to. When I did, I was soon woken by a text.

I slowly adjusted my eyes to the darkness of my room and glanced at my phone, still glowing with its sudden activity. I threw off my duvet and hurled myself towards my desk. It was covered in revision notes for science. My life was now all about revision. No one cared about who was seeing whom any longer; it was just about how much revision you had done. I suppose it made a change from a few months ago, when it was all about which college you were going to for Year Twelve. This obsession with our future meant that my mobile sometimes went into a sort of hibernation mode, as everyone was too busy to text. Every so often I would check to see if my mobile was still working. The last time Mum had caught me and had laughed. That was when I became convinced that it was some sort of conspiracy between the government, parents, and mobile phone networks, to get us to revise.

Tanisha: *Grma told me you're going to do the puberty rites. R U crazy?*

That girl had no respect for time difference! She just acted like we were in the same time zone!

Me: *No. It might be interesting.*
Tanisha: *Interesting? I'm the flipping American one here and even I can see this isn't going to make you any more Ghanaian!*
Me: *Sod off! BTW stop msgin me between 1–3 A.M. London time!*
Tanisha: *U answered. No one forced U. I'll call u l8r.*

Great, just what I needed! Somehow I had to be out of the house when Tanisha called the landline. She's my cousin and a grilling from her could make a grown-up feel like a naughty child. Dad said she'd always been like that, and that Auntie Jennifer had reckoned Tanisha would make a great lawyer, even when she was a little girl. She was right: Tanisha was in her second year of a law degree in the USA and her advocacy skills were way too advanced for me.

I sighed. I had to find out why everyone was going nuts over this ceremony and I was getting seriously worried, but I was too embarrassed to admit I didn't have a clue about what to expect.

My phone beeped again. What was it with nocturnal people! I got next to no texts and then they all came at once. It was like waiting for a bus!

Nelson: *Wanna revise Monday nite?*

Me: *Sure. How come you're up so late?*

Nelson: *Just got back from my cousin's party. Soz if I woke U. I'll meet U outside your school – I finish early. X*

Me: *Sure. C U then.*

Whatever. The ceremony details could wait.

Chapter 4
Good Kiss vs Bad Kiss

Me: *Get to a computer pronto. We need IM convo, like yesterday.*

Bharti: *OMG! Has something huge happened?*

Me: *Don't be totally illogical. Of course it HAS!*

When I got home at about six p.m, Delphy was already in her room doing her homework or up to something. It was hard to tell nowadays – either way she'd make sure she had a book that resembled a text book in front of her alongside an exercise book on the desk. I was impressed: apart from her earlier indiscretion involving those bags from New York, she had managed to keep her promise to Mum and Dad about not getting involved in any mini business ventures before secondary school.

'Hey, Dad,' I said, as he walked in carrying a whole load of papers.

'Makeeda, do you think you could order a pizza or something tonight? I told your mum I'd cook, but I've got to go through this lot.'

'Where's Mum?'

'She's gone to help Grace. So can you sort out dinner?'

'Sure, Dad!' Delphina shouted from the top of the stairs.

'He asked me!' I protested.

'Don't argue about it – just sort it out!' Dad said, before disappearing into the dining room.

Delphina rolled her eyes. It was the same every six months. Dad would have to sort out the paperwork for the garage before meeting his accountant and would get into a bad mood. (Mum was the same around Ofsted inspections. She was already deputy head of the history department and she'd only been there just over a year.) The good news, though, was that Dad wouldn't notice if I didn't start revising immediately. My phone beeped.

Bharti: *Makeeda? I'm waiting. I've just had to sneak a plate of 'supper' from the warden.*

Me: *Seconds!!*

Bharti was away on a revision course that meant that she was excused from school for a few days. Our school was only letting her do it because they didn't want anything affecting their position in the league tables. I quickly logged on.

BoredBharti: Well?

Diva: OMG, I just spent a weird revision session with Nelson.

BoredBharti: Did you and Nelson get any revision done? ;)

Diva: Sort of. BUT, have I told you about the puberty ceremony?

BoredBharti: What puberty ceremony?

I quickly filled her in about my discovery that, in one phone call, I had agreed to undergo a traditional ceremony.

BoredBharti: Wait, so instead of hanging up on your nana you just did the yeah, yeah, thing?

Diva: Yup!

BoredBharti: Ha HAAAAAAAAAAAAAAAAAAAAAAAAAAAAAAAAA

Diva: Oh thanks!

BoredBharti: Sorry.

Diva: Don't tell me, the 'a' key got stuck on the keyboard!

BoredBharti: It didn't. I was just being cruel. Makeeda, U can be a real thicko sometimes. Just tell them you don't want to do the ceremony.

Diva: It's not that simple.

It wasn't. It was too late to back out now – I would look stupid. I couldn't bear the thought of the smug look on Afua's face. Plus, a bit of me didn't want to disappoint everyone.

BoredBharti: Yes it is.

Diva: Bharti, it's not! U can't tell me to not do some-thing traditional, after all the things you do for your culture and religion!

BoredBharti: Whatever! So why bother telling me in the first place? You seem to have all the answers already!

She was right. I needed her and I was being mean.

Diva: Sorry. I just wish I could hop on a bus and see you and we could pretend to revise in that coffee shop in Harrow.

BoredBharti: LOL I miss U too. I have only made two mates here. It's so lame. Every1 is more serious than I am about revision.

Diva: What? That's totally illogical!

BoredBharti: I know! So what happened with Nelson?

Diva: Nothing much. It was OK, I guess.

I had met Nelson earlier that evening to revise, but we spent most of our time messing around. Not like before when we'd kiss, but literally messing around, like chucking bits of paper at each other and getting asked to leave the library in front of everyone. It was beginning to feel more like we were mates. It didn't help that when we left we bumped into Nick and his new friend Sanari.

BoredBharti: So what does Nick's girlfriend look like?

Diva:	Why do you think she's his girlfriend??
BoredBharti:	CHILL! I meant as in girl (space) friend. So what does she look like?
Diva:	Gorgeous. She has almond-shaped eyes, really great dress sense and her jewellery looked real. I hate her.
BoredBharti:	Huh? Now who's being totally illogical? You can't hate someone you just met!
Diva:	Well, she is doing her A-levels and was trying to give me advice on my GCSEs like I was some kind of thicko!
BoredBharti:	Wait a minute – you're not a thicko??
Diva:	Hey!
BoredBharti:	Makeeda, I'm really sorry, but I can't stay too long. The other class finishes in ten minutes so there'll be a huge queue to use the PCs. Seriously, it's like there were free iPods sprouting out of the PCs or something.
Diva:	LOL! Oh soz. I 4got U weren't home.

Delphina was yelling at me about dinner, but I didn't care; there was something I still had to run by Bharti.

'Delphy! Just get whatever you know I like and wouldn't cuss you over!'

'Huh?' Delphy said.

'Choose wisely, little sis!' I said and closed my bedroom door.

I told Bharti about what had happened after Nelson and I left Nick and Sanari. Nelson and I did our usual thing, where

I spent some time avoiding a kiss then finally gave in. For a while it had felt like we weren't as affectionate with each other as before. Sometimes we'd see each other and the closest we'd get to kissing was an awkward hug. This time we kissed, but I didn't expect the strange feeling that kissing him left me with.

BoredBharti: What do you mean, it felt weird?

Diva: It just did.

BoredBharti: What, like kissing cousins – just plain wrong weird, or you have bad breath, please introduce some mouthwash to your oral hygiene routine weird?

Diva: Both.

BoredBharti: Oh.

Diva: Oh? Is that all you can say?

BoredBharti: Soz. Is just that um . . .

Diva: BHARTI?

BoredBharti: Don't flipping CAPS me!

Diva: Soz.

BoredBharti: Well . . . bad kisses always mean bad things. I mean, didn't Judas use a kiss to betray Jesus?

Diva: Yeah, I suppose so.

BoredBharti: You're meant to be Christian, you should KNOW!

Diva: Oh shut up, are you telling me you know all the deities in Hinduism?

BoredBharti: No, but we are sitting our religious studies

	exam in a month and Hinduism, Judaism, Christianity and Islam are in the exam! So back to the kiss thing. Heard of the kiss of death?
Diva:	Yeah. OHMIGOD!!
BoredBharti:	What is it with U and CAPS?
Diva:	So you think Nelson's either going to betray me or kill me? LOL!
BoredBharti:	Ha flipping haaa!

I knew exactly what Bharti meant though, but it felt strange to be finally saying it. This had been a long road with an obvious end. Nelson and I were over.

Diva:	That was our last kiss, wasn't it?
BoredBharti:	Yeah. Sorry, Makeeda. The good news is that, according to your star sign, new beginnings only happen when stale bread is thrown out.
Diva:	What?
BoredBharti:	Sorry, I got sidetracked by a bit of stale bread near my keyboard. It says, 'New beginnings only start when we acknowledge the stale relationships we have. Don't let the green-eyed monster prevent you from making new friends.'
Diva:	That's interesting. I wonder if it's talking about Nelson or Nick.
BoredBharti:	Nick?
Diva:	Oh, I meant his friend Sanari, dunno why I said him?! So what does your one say?

BoredBharti: *It says, 'You've been struck by Cupid's arrow, but beware: this could be a romantic roller-coaster. Enjoy the ride for now!*

Diva: *Well? Anything to tell me? Who hit you with Cupid's arrow?*

BoredBharti: *Yeah, right, like that's gonna happen to me on a revision course! That's totally illogical! Listen, I'm getting evils from people in the queue. I have to go. Catch up when I get back.*

Diva: *Yeah, thanks. BTW how did you smuggle your mobile in? I thought they banned them on the course?*

BoredBharti: *They did. I went old-school and hid it in my sock, which meant faking a sprained ankle. About five of us got away with it. I'm in the cool crowd, Makeeda. Bye!! X*

Talking to Bharti had made me realise a lot of things. But first things first: I needed to tell Mum and Dad the truth about the puberty ceremony. I couldn't go on pretending I was really excited to do it, when it freaked me out and could potentially ruin my holiday.

I walked into the living room to find Mum and Dad sitting on the sofa. Mum must have got back early and calmed Dad down. She had her legs across Dad's lap. I was just grateful they weren't kissing. Recently they'd been all over each other, ever since they'd started going to the gym together. When your own love life wasn't exactly high on the old kissometer, the last thing you needed to see were PDAs (Parental Displays of Affection). Bharti and I both agreed it messed with your head. I mean, we were living proof it went on so we really didn't need to see it.

'You OK, Makeeda?' Dad asked.

'Um . . . I need to tell you something.'

'You look so worried . . . Dad began.

Mum immediately sat up and nudged Dad to be quiet. Their relaxed faces suddenly changed to what I called high-level alert. It's like their bodies went rigid into a pre-explosion state of anger, where the words from my lips could potentially act as a trigger. I hadn't been on the receiving end of one of those in a while now but it didn't make this any easier for me.

'I . . . '

'Makeeda, you're not . . . ' Dad began.

'What?' I prompted.

'. . . with child?' he said, removing his glasses.

'With what?' I said, horrified. Actually, I wasn't sure what was more shocking; the fact that Dad couldn't say pregnant or that he thought I would be!

'It's OK, we can work things out . . .' Mum began.

'Nooo! Ohmigod! Why would you think that? You always said I was too young to . . . Seriously, why would you think that?'

'Oh thank God!' Mum interrupted.

I actually heard Dad sigh in relief. This was the problem with all those newspaper articles about teenage pregnancies. Mum and Dad always got a bit weird after reading them.

Bharti had told me that, when her parents had sat her and her brother Tejas down for 'the chat', it had been so embarrassing that Tejas had walked out saying he'd ask their cousin Deeps, and she said she'd ask Meena.

'I can't be a glamorous granny. I haven't finished the yummy mummy part yet!' Mum said.

'Hmm . . . if you say so, but I did see a grey hair —' Dad began.

'Where?' Mum said alarmed.

Dad started laughing.

'Oh very funny!' Mum said, poking him.

I coughed loudly. I could see a PDA coming on and I was too far from the door to escape.

'So Makeeda, what's the problem?'

'The puberty ceremony,'

'Ahh . . . Your nana probably railroaded you into it, didn't she?' Mum said.

'Well, not exactly. I just sort of did the yeah, yeah thing – the line was pretty bad . . .'

'Makeeda!' Dad said, shocked. 'That's no way to treat your grandmother!'

'Like you haven't done it before,' Mum said to Dad.

This was a new one. They never discussed stuff like that in English. Mum and Dad had seriously altered their parental style recently.

'Well, just concentrate on your revision for now and you can decide later about the ceremony.'

'Thanks, Mum,' I said, walking out.

At least Mum and Dad weren't too bothered if I didn't go ahead with the puberty ceremony. I actually felt lighter for having told them. It was one less thing to worry about.

Chapter 5

The Unexpected

I jumped out of the shower and headed to my room. It felt great to have the house to myself for a change! Well, almost. Dad was around, but he didn't really count when it came to competing for the bathroom or mirror. I'd managed to squeeze in some English lit revision after finally finishing my science coursework. My ntoma was hung up on my wardrobe door freshly ironed. We had to leave at seven p.m. for Aunt Grace's Ghana Independence party. Recently we'd been getting really good with our timekeeping. Unfortunately, this just meant we were early everywhere, as everyone else was on GMT (Ghanaian Mean Time) and running at least two hours late!

Aunt Grace had organised a Ghanaian Independence Day

party but it was taking place two months after 6th March because she couldn't book a hall in time. She wanted to raise money for children's charities in the UK and Ghana. Unlike all the other parties, this one was aimed at young people. Afua and I were more than a bit suspicious at this, especially when Aunt Grace said, 'It will be good for all of you young Ghanaians to get to know each other.' There was a glint in her eye.

The only upside was that there were guaranteed to be some celebrities there, including a premiership football player and a TV presenter. When their agents replied that they'd be happy to attend and even be our MCs for the night, we were in shock for days! It meant we could up the ticket price by five pounds. Their presence also meant that everyone our age would show up and not think it was just another function for oldies, masquerading as a party for Ghanaian youth. Afua and I helped Aunt Grace organise the event in between our revision, but Mum and Dad took over the really involved stuff a month ago.

When Aunt Grace ran the DJ list past us, Afua and I began laughing hysterically. There was no way a DJ who only played pop and didn't have a clue about the latest download hits would work at this party. We told Aunt Grace she needed to find someone with a music library that had the latest UK urban music, and Hip-Life, an African version of hip-hop. I would've suggested Nelson, but he wasn't allowed to DJ until his last exam had been sat. So we had a DJ from the local African radio station.

'Makeeda, you've got twenty minutes to get ready!'

'OK, Dad,' I yelled back. Twenty flipping minutes indeed!

There was no way I was going to be ready in twenty minutes! It took me, on average, ten to decide which jewellery to wear and then another twenty to apply my make-up. This could include tinted moisturiser, but Mum forbade me to wear foundation till I was twenty. She has a theory that too much make-up when you're young causes wrinkles later on. I didn't mind too much as I was nearly sixteen and she'd has eased up and actually shown me how to apply it properly. She gave me a funny look the last time I put eye-shadow on, but it was hardly my fault if it didn't look quite right – she should have shown me how to do it ages ago.

'Makeeda, ten minutes!'

'No way, Dad! Only two minutes have gone by!'

'Are you arguing with me?'

I wanted to scream yes, but it came out as a mumble that turned into a no.

An hour later, Dad and I arrived at the venue – a hall in Harrow. It had recently been refurbished and had cream walls and wood flooring, with a stage on the left and huge windows which had been decorated with Ghanaian flags. There were tables near the stage for the quiz later and some extra chairs and tables dotted around the room. All the tables had balloons floating in Ghana's colours – red, green and yellow.

As soon as Mum spotted me, she gave me a plastic apron and told me to help Delphina and Afua sort out the buffet table. The DJ had already arrived and began playing some

Hip-Life as we finished decorating the room. When the music suddenly changed to one of Dad and Aunt Grace's favourite tunes, 'Sika', I turned to see Dad dancing on the stage with a beer in his hand, trying to be funny. Delphy and I cringed, feeling slightly relieved that there were only two guests in the hall. Dad's old-man boogie dance moves were enough to stop anyone else from hitting the dance floor. Luckily, within a minute Mum had got Dad helping her at the door.

'So glad Mum's here,' Delphy said, attaching a banner to the stage.

'Me too. Where's Afua?'

'She's gone to get changed. You know *they're* here,' Delphina said, excitedly.

'What Eddie and Faith?' I asked, looking about for the celebrities.

'Yeah, they got here just before you did, but they're changing in the other room.'

'Ohmigod, what are they like?'

'How would I know? Mum and Aunt Grace won't let anyone near them!' Delphina shrugged.

Within half an hour, the room was half full. There were lots of people my age and a handful of adults. I had just finished helping Aunt Grace in the kitchen when I heard someone calling my name. I turned around to find Jordan, Nelson's friend, grinning back at me. He was dressed in a suit.

'What are you doing here?'

'My cousin invited me.' Jordan smiled.

'I never knew you were Ghanaian!'

'Yeah, my Dad's half Irish and Ghanaian, and my Mum's Russian.'

'Seriously?' I was shocked.

'Nah, I just wanted to see Eddie Gambia, innit?' Jordan said.

'You joker!' I said, hitting him.

'Hey, don't mess with the suit. How did you get a footballer like him to come anyway?'

'Oh, Aunt Grace just emailed his agent over a hundred times.'

'And that was it?'

'Yeah, but it can't have hurt that his aunt and my aunt's best mate went to Achimota School together. I can't believe you lied about being Ghanaian.'

'No, I didn't. *Mi papa ye Ghana ni!*'

'Ohmigod, you speak Twi!'

'I can only say that, but I speak Russian fluently.'

'How come you never told me?'

'You never asked!' he said.

He had a point. I knew Jordan was mixed race, but it never crossed my mind that he could be Ghanaian, too. But, the conversations I had with Jordan didn't always make a lot of sense – that was why he was fun to be around.

'Makeeda,' he said, placing a hand on my shoulder, 'I came to look for talent, so I hope you invited some model types.'

'Jordan!'

'I'm serious. A man like me can't be single for too long – it's like a crime against nature or something.'

I laughed. 'You're unnatural all right!'

'So, can you hook me up with Faith Osei-Mensah?'

'You want me to hook you up with a famous TV presenter?'

'Yeah, she might like the look of a young, sophisticated man in his prime.'

'Makeeda!' Aunt Grace called.

'I have to go. See you later.'

I was impressed that Jordan was here and it made me wonder why Nelson couldn't be bothered to attend. Telling me that he 'didn't fancy it' just made me ask myself if he had stopped caring about us completely. Weirdly enough, I wasn't too bothered.

Aunt Grace was dressed in black and white Kente. She looked fantastic – her hair and nails were done and her jewellery complemented her outfit.

'Right, Faith and Eddie are here, so your mum will introduce them and we'll start off with the quiz, then have a bite to eat, and then dance or do what you youngsters call dancing,' she said, smiling warmly at me.

'OK, Auntie.' I shrugged.

'I just need you to find Afua and collect our VIP guests from the other room.'

'Whaaaaaaaaaaaaaaaaaaat? Me?' My hands started shaking.

'Yes, you and Afua. Come on, Makeeda, they're just people,' Aunt Grace added.

Yeah, right! A woman who has interviewed rock stars, politicians and everyone in between, and a man who scored the winning goal in a Premiership match for Arsenal a few weeks ago! Well, at least Dad would be proud. Mum would have to keep Dad away from his football hero, or he would embarrass himself and the family with all his gushing.

'Hey, Makeeda!' Afua said, rushing up to me. She was wearing a blue dress, the same colour as my ntoma and had a turquoise Kente shawl across her shoulders.

'You look great!' she said, grinning.

'Thanks. Come on, let's get this over and done with.'

'Nervous?' she asked.

'Yeah, aren't you?'

'Put it this way: pretty soon we'll be sitting our GCSEs. It's all about perspective.'

'True,' I said, smiling.

Afua and I greeted our VIPs and walked them into the hall. I liked Faith: she was really sweet to me and gave me her lip-gloss (unused) which made Afua jealous. She kept saying, 'Ohmigod, I even got her a glass of water earlier!' As for Eddie, he was just as gorgeous as he seemed on TV and really friendly and charming.

It was soon time for the quiz. Afua and I hadn't helped Aunt Grace with it – we wanted to enter it ourselves.

I looked around for Nick. My quiz partner was late! I was about to give up and join Jordan's group when Nick walked in with Sanari.

'Who is that?' Afua asked.

'Nick and Sanari.'

'Wow!' Afua said. 'He looks better than the last time I saw him. Is that his girlfriend?'

'No!' I said angrily.

'Hey, no need to get snappy,' Afua said.

'I —'

'Hey, sorry we're late,' Nick interrupted.

'It was my fault – I couldn't decide what to wear,' Sanari added, smiling beside him.

I couldn't help but stare at her immaculate face and clothing. Her hijab was a pale pink that complemented her skin tone and made the pink polka dots in her beige-coloured dress stand out. The dress looked familiar. I suddenly remembered Tanisha emailing a picture of it to me last month. It was designer!

'Yeah, that's OK,' I said, faking a smile. It wasn't. Why on earth had Nick brought Ms Gorgeous? Was I wrong? Was Sanari his new girlfriend?

Within minutes, Afua had taken Sanari to her table, whilst Nick and I settled into our quiz mode. The people who had entered the quiz were sitting on the ten tables closest to the stage. The questions came thick and fast with Faith and Eddie cracking loads of jokes in between. I'd been so relieved when they'd agreed to be quizmasters instead of Mum and Dad, which would have been *too* embarrassing.

It soon came to a dead heat, with Nick and I competing against Jordan and his cousin, and two other guests. Our next challenge was to write a list of the Akan names next to the correct days of the week. According to Akan custom, everyone is given a name depending on the day they are born. Mine is Amma because I was born on a Saturday, but I never use that name.

'Makeeda, how well do you know this?' Nick whispered.

'Are you kidding? All I can think of is my name and Delphy's.'

'I only know Kofi, because that's mine and I was born on a Friday,' said Nick, flushing with embarrassment. 'I know it looks bad but I spent more time with my Polish gran than Nana-Betty, so I don't really know this stuff.'

'Oh well, we'll just have to work out the rest.' I shrugged.

I'd never really considered what it would be like having to learn two languages on top of English. I only had Twi to learn yet mine was awful.

We sat there, writing and rewriting all the other names until we were happy.

Eventually we handed our paper in.

After a tense few minutes of Aunt Grace, Faith and Eddie checking the results, it was announced that Nick and I were in the final with the other guests after the interval. Jordan looked gutted, but still wished us luck and used the interval to introduce himself to Faith. By this time everyone was eating, drinking, and chatting to each other. There was a crowd of people around Eddie wanting to take photographs with him, and Faith was chatting to some of the girls. We watched as Jordan skilfully managed to divert Faith away from the crowd, into having a one-on-one conversation with him.

'Is he doing what I think he is?' Nick asked.

'Yep, he wanted me to hook him up with her.'

'He's a bit of a fantasist, isn't he?'

'Yep!' I said, laughing. 'I mean, there is no way Faith would dump that Hollywood actor for a kid from Harrow.'

'No, but you've got to respect a guy who tries.'

'Seriously? He is flirting with a woman twelve years his senior.'

'Makeeda, it's called taking a risk. People do it all the time when they want someone badly enough.' Nick smiled.

The DJ stopped the music and Aunt Grace asked everyone to find a seat for the remaining part of the competition.

Faith had to be rescued by Eddie, who physically steered Jordan away from her so that the quiz could resume.

'In which year did Queen Yaa-Asantewaa fight the British?' Eddie asked. 'Is it A: 1912, B: 1900, or C: 1800?

That was easy. 1900. Unfortunately, the other team knew the answer too.

'OK, what was the name of the Ghana's first president?' asked Faith.

Dr Kwame Nkrumah, Nick wrote down.

Both teams got that right too.

'You are killing me! How bright are you guys?' Faith said.

'Ohmigod, who *are* they?' I whispered, staring at our competitors.

'Makeeda, we're up against a guy who goes to Harrow Boys School and is in their top five per cent and a girl who did her GCSEs a year early.'

'No way!'

'Yep, makes your essay and my smoothie business seem like pretty small achievements.'

Nick was a bit like Delphy – an entrepeneur – and a few years ago he developed a smoothie business, delivering drinks to the local cafés and corner shops in Edgware and Harrow. Eventually he sold the entire thing to a posh chain of sandwich shops in London, making enough money to put him and his brother through university.

'Ahh . . . man, and I thought you were the only brainbox I knew,' I said.

'Shut up, I still am!' Nick said, tickling me.

'Not any more!' I giggled.

Aunt Grace coughed to get our attention and I noticed that we suddenly had an audience of my parents, Afua, Jordan, Sanari and Delphina. Delphina was glaring at me. I guess her crush on Nick was still going strong. I could also see our competitors staring at us.

'You don't think they heard us?' I asked Nick.

'Nah. That's just a competitive stare. They're trying to psyche us out,' he replied.

Anxiously, we waited for the next question.

'Wow, we have some real intelligent Ghanaians here today, so we need another question,' Eddie said with a grin. 'Name the man who wanted to sit on The Golden Stool . . . '

I immediately grabbed the pen from Nick's hand and wrote *Governor Hodgson*, remembering the detail from my essay last year.

'Hopefully this will be the final check!' Eddie said as Faith quickly checked our answers.

'And the winners, by one point, are Makeeda and Nick!' Eddie and Faith announced.

A huge cheer erupted in the hall. Nick hugged me tightly.

When we pulled away something weird happened. It was like our faces were drawn to each other and we nearly kissed.

It was so quick, so fleeting, that I almost didn't believe it had actually happened. Immediately, I gasped and we pulled apart really quickly. By this time everyone else had focussed on Faith and Eddie's hunt for our prize, so no one was looking our way. This didn't make any sense: why would Nick and I want to kiss each other? Me and Nick? This was totally illogical!

Chapter 6

About Doing the Right Thing . . .

I had spent the days following Aunt Grace's party in a state of shock. I kept thinking about Nick and how we had nearly kissed. At first, I couldn't concentrate enough to get any revision done, but then the exams began and I went into hyper revision mode, where I ate, slept, and breathed my GCSEs. It was weird being at school and not feeling confident enough about how that day's exam had gone to hang out with everyone and discuss it afterwards. Even Bharti seemed to be in an exam haze – we barely spoke to each other. She was always in a rush to be somewhere else.

It was only when there were just five days to go until my

final exam that I felt I could relax slightly and think about Nick again. Since Aunt Grace's party I'd only seen him once and that was to go over any last-minute maths problems I had before my exam. He seemed happy to see me, but it was like nothing had happened. He seemed to only want to talk about maths. So I tried to forget about it, but I couldn't.

Did Nick fancy me? The question of whether I fancied him was now redundant. I knew my feelings for him had altered. Before he came round for the maths lesson, I changed outfits six times. Delphina thought I must have been meeting Nelson, so she was stunned to see Nick walk through our front door.

People didn't accidentally almost kiss. I also knew that I wasn't one of those girls who could claim to fancy two guys at the same time, because I definitely hadn't fancied Nelson in ages and now couldn't stop thinking about Nick.

That's when I began to feel terrible about Nelson. What was I doing? He had sent sweet texts wishing me luck in my exams, but all I could feel was guilt. I had a secret. I knew something he didn't and I knew I couldn't keep it from him much longer. I hadn't wanted to split up with Nelson before or during our exams, that would be too mean and besides, I didn't want to be known as the girl who messed up Nelson's GCSEs.

It would have helped if I'd had someone to talk to, but Bharti barely responded to my request for a chat, saying she was busy that afternoon, and that left Tanisha.

I really didn't want to chat to Tanisha, but Mum had been bugging me to call her, as she'd left loads of messages. I knew it would mean listening to her go on and on about the puberty ceremony. I wasn't wrong. It was even worse using Skype. At least, if I was on the phone, I could cut the call short by telling her that I needed to do something that required both hands, but with Skype it was like having a hands-free phone. I was just grateful our webcam was broken.

'Makeeda, I don't get it. Why?' Tanisha said in her American/British accent.

No one quite knew or understood how Tanisha had managed to maintain parts of her British accent, despite living in the States since she was twelve. Her dad moved out there after her mum, Auntie Jennifer, had died. Auntie Jennifer was Mum's sister.

'It doesn't matter, because I haven't made up my mind yet, anyway,' I responded.

'Yeah, but why exactly would you even consider doing this ceremony?'

'Why not?'

'It's archaic, Makeeda. It's got nothing to do with your life.'

It was strange – even though I had walked blindly into this situation, part of me was warming to the idea. I mean, it was part of a tradition that all my female ancestors had undergone, so what was so wrong with me doing a version of it now?

'I just haven't made up my mind yet, Tanisha.'

'OOOOOH you're so stubborn! Just admit it. You have no idea what it means and you're freaking out inside!' Tanisha screamed.

'I think you may have broken the speakers on my PC, so thanks,' I said, making a mental note to always adjust the speaker volume if Tanisha and I were going to have a Skype chat. She was right: I had no idea what was involved in a puberty ceremony. I mean, I had tried to find out but it seemed to be shrouded in mystery. Mum said it was a celebration recognising the transition from being a girl to becoming a woman, and that I'd be doing activities that reflected this transition. Then we got interrupted so I never got a chance to discuss it with her again. I had even tried to Google it, but then I couldn't find much except boring academic essays that I had no time to read because of my RG.

'You're being dumb, Makeeda.'

'Whatever.'

After a minute's silence, that felt more like ten, Tanisha spoke.

'So how's Nick?'

'Umm, OK . . . '

'What does that mean?'

I told Tanisha everything that had happened.

'Well, I hope you're not going to lie to yourself about this, too.'

'What do you mean?'

'It's obvious you fancy Nick, so you'd better split up with Nelson.'

'What?'

'Come on, Makeeda! You can't seriously tell me that all those times you got excited about Nick showing up at your place or when he gave you private tuition for free, there was no chemistry!'

'Well . . .'

'Oh, don't pretend!'

'OK fine, but what about Sanari?'

'Listen, you free yourself up first and the rest will fall into place.'

'Seriously?'

'Yeah. Look, Makeeda, I'm guessing that you'd already thought about splitting up with Nelson, before the almost-kiss with Nick.'

'Wow!' I said, shocked. It was like Tanisha had been in my head.

'Yes, I know. I'm real good at this stuff.'

'At least you're not smug with it, eh?' I replied.

'Shut up and listen for a change!' Tanisha said. 'All I wanted to say was, don't let this put you off your revision. No guy is worth sabotaging your future over.'

'Oh, I know that.'

'Makeeda, I'm being serious. None of this stuff is as important as you passing your GCSEs.'

'You sound like Mum and Dad.'

'I know, but put it this way: you know how smart Nick is, do you think he'd wanna be dating a klutz and . . .'

'I'm not a klutz! I didn't mean to drop that bottle of perfume in the shop.'

Last summer I was in a department store when I picked up a tester and dropped it as I handed it back to the sales assistant. I was on the phone to Tanisha at the time and she'd been calling me a klutz since.

'Sorry, I meant a thicko with no GCSEs,' Tanisha said, laughing.

'OK, you have a point.'

'I know I do,' Tanisha said, and I could hear the smile in her voice. 'So good luck, and get back to that revision!'

I wasn't sure what was worse: having a smug know-it-all cousin, or knowing that in a short time I'd have to split up with Nelson. I decided to do it immediately. I knew that he had already finished his exams. I had one left, but that didn't matter – I just needed to get this sorted out.

Nelson was walking towards me in a T-shirt and shorts. I was dressed in a denim skirt and a T-shirt. I had changed three times, because I didn't want to appear really awful or too good. What should you wear when you're about to split up with your boyfriend? There was nothing helpful online, and none of my friends who would know were available, so it just left me, my wardrobe and a mirror, and that day I wasn't sure of anything.

We met at the bus stop and walked into Stanmore Park. For a while we didn't really say much; we just swung idly on the swings until a family approached and the kids asked if they could use them.

As we walked down the hill, I plucked up what little courage I had. 'Nelson, I need to say something important.'

'OK, but can we just walk a bit more? There's a café along here somewhere,' he said.

'Sure.' I shrugged.

Splitting up with Nelson took less time than I thought it would.

'I just don't feel the same way I did when we first met,' I said, after we'd got some drinks and sat down.

He didn't act surprised or anything – he just questioned me. 'What does that mean?'

'It means I see you more as . . . family.' As soon as I said it, I regretted it. Tanisha had once told me the friend/family thing was the worst thing anyone could ever tell you. It basically meant that you could never ever see that person as being anything else in your life, because there was a huge fault in the way they looked, spoke or behaved.

'Oh great! You change your mind about how you feel about me and that's it, we're done?'

I stared at him. I could see how angry he was becoming, but there was no way I could pretend to be happy with him when I had stronger feelings for Nick.

'Are you telling me that you're happy the way things are?' I asked.

'No, I just know that sometimes you have to work at things, Makeeda.'

'I can't do that.'

'No, you *won't* do it, because you don't think we're worth saving. There's a difference.'

He was right. But I also knew we were finished a long time ago.

'Nelson, don't put all of this on me. You haven't exactly made a huge effort to make things work!' I said, accusingly.

'I've had exams.'

'So have I! But not every day since January!' I shot back at him.

Oh no. I was awful at this. I really didn't mean to say that. I watched as a cloud grew across his features. He sank back into his seat, with a mixture of shock and anger.

'January?' he whispered.

For what felt like ten minutes, he barely looked at me and concentrated on fiddling with the straw in his empty milkshake glass. I just sat there, wishing I could learn to stop letting go of words that damaged their listeners. I longed to be one of the passers-by on the other side of the window, instead of sitting opposite Nelson in silence.

'That's a long time to feel like that, Makeeda. I thought we were more honest with each other.'

I wasn't sure what to say. Should I confirm this and risk hurting him even more? Or just lie?

'I'm sorry,' I said instead.

'No, you don't get it. I felt like things went off between us in January, too.' He wouldn't meet my eyes.

'What?' This confirmed everything. It looked like I wasn't the only one in denial.

'Well, why didn't you —?' I spluttered.

'I just hoped we'd work it out. You know, like we've done before?' Nelson interrupted.

'I don't think that's possible. I mean, it's not like you love me or anything.'

'I do,' he whispered. 'I really like you, Makeeda.'

'Oh,' I gasped. I didn't want Nelson to tell me that. I wanted this to be over.

'I love you, Makeeda. But you're right – it's more like a really special friend than a girlfriend. And that's not really fair on either of us, is it?'

'I guess not.'

It was weird hearing my own words thrown back in my face. Nelson and I were breaking up. I couldn't bring myself to tell him the whole truth, so I never told him about my feelings for Nick. We were finished long before the almost-kiss with Nick, so what would be the point of hurting him more? But it was odd, admitting that we had both known things hadn't been right. And it hurt when we said goodbye that Nelson could wish me luck 'with everything', as it meant that he had already decided not to be part of my future.

I really wanted to hug him tightly and tell him that he was a fantastic boyfriend, but it was too awkward. He kissed me, barely allowing any part of himself to touch me, other than the briefest brush of his lips against mine, but even then he acted like he'd been burned and stepped back. As he walked away, I saw him wiping his eyes quickly. He was hurt. I desperately wanted him to turn around, but he didn't. If he had, he would have seen my tear-stained cheeks.

No one had ever told me that doing the right thing would hurt that much. I wished they had. I wished I could've been more prepared for the sudden raw feeling of grief.

I couldn't go straight home, so I took the train into central London and hoped that hiding behind my science revision guide would stop people staring at my tears.

I texted Bharti, praying for a reply – she had been distant ever since her revision course but I had thought that was because of our exams. Now we only had one exam to go, I thought that I'd be able to see her, but she still seemed busy. It had been hard enough seeing her before our exams, when she was going to dance classes twice a week. Now it felt like she was more of an imaginary friend.

Bharti: *Soz, I can't meet. Got relatives round.*
Me: *Call me tonight. I really need 2 tlk.*
Bharti: *Sure. X*

I sighed. I guessed it could wait. As I walked towards TopShop I saw a girl who looked like Bharti. I almost called her name out, but I stopped as I saw her heading into a shoe shop. As I got closer, I noticed she was holding hands with a boy. I followed them and my breath caught in my throat. This girl didn't just look like Bharti. It *was* Bharti! Another huge tear rolled down my cheek and I went straight back to the station and headed home. Why did she lie to me?

It suddenly made sense. She had barely contacted me since returning from her revision course, and now I knew why. Bharti had a boyfriend. But why wouldn't she want me to know?

Chapter 7

Honest Secrets

The final GCSE exam of my life was over. I watched as the invigilator collected the last paper. There was a mixture of anticipation and relief in the air as well as sweat. It was boiling in the gym – the heating had come on half an hour before the end. The rules meant we had to finish the exam anyway, but I reckoned I could use it as an excuse if I didn't get a good grade in that paper. It seemed to take ages for us to be dismissed as we had to file out of the gym in rows.

'Hey, Makeeda, how did it go?' Bharti raced up to me.

'OK,' I said. I was still furious with her, so I just carried on walking.

'Hey, what's up? I tried calling you a few days ago, but Delphy said you were busy.'

'Yeah, so?' I said curtly.

'What have I done wrong now?'

'Bharti, why didn't you tell me about your boyfriend?'

'Shhh! Ohmigod, how did you find out?' Bharti said, grabbing me by the arm.

'Ouch, that hurts!' I said, pulling away. 'Last week. You know, the day you said you had relatives round? Well, I saw you on Oxford Street.'

'Makeeda, I'm sorry, but I just couldn't tell you. Can we go for a walk or something?' Bharti asked.

She kept looking over her shoulder and I realised she was worried that the other girls might have overheard us.

'Fine, but you'd better give me a decent excuse,' I replied.

We walked from school all the way through Harrow and eventually headed towards Bharti's house. The boy I had seen Bharti with was her boyfriend, Rafi. She had met him on the revision course she went on. She'd been lying to me all this time.

'Technically it's an omission, Makeeda. A huge omission, but not a lie.'

'Bharti, you're not really in a position to get all funny and technical with me. The fact is, you never told me about the biggest thing to happen to you in ages! Don't you trust me?'

'Makeeda, of course I trust you! I just didn't want to put you in an awkward position, if my parents cornered you.'

'Why would they?' I questioned.

'Rafi isn't Hindu.'

'Uh huh.' I stared at Bharti waiting for a huge bombshell.

'I'm Hindu and he's not. His name is Rafi!' Bharti said.

'So?'

'Makeeda, I'm a Hindu girl, dating a Muslim boy. Why don't you get this?'

I was puzzled. I mean, I'd heard some of the other girls in my year mention it as a big deal, but I never thought Bharti felt the same way.

'Is it really that big a deal?'

'Yeah, I doubt Gayatri would speak to me again.'

'Your auntie?'

'Yeah.'

Bharti's mum had a younger sister who was about thirty and really opinionated.

I remembered Tejas being caught kissing his Polish girlfriend, in Harrow bus station, by one of his aunt's friends. His parents hadn't been bothered about it, but when his aunt confronted him he told her that he was never going to date a 'nice Indian girl'. Although, according to Bharti, his current girlfriend was someone their aunt would really approve of, he still went to crazy lengths to avoid being seen with her. Tejas didn't want his aunt in his business – he was actually pleased when his girlfriend's family moved to St Albans, as his aunt's spies were all in Harrow.

Tejas had once stopped me from going into their home because Gayatri was there. She hated me being best friends with Bharti and I hated the fact that she was Bharti's aunt. Once when Bharti's parents were away and she was in charge, she kept asking me odd questions about what Mum and Dad did for a living. It felt like she was trying to work out whether I was good enough to be her niece's friend. Aunt Grace told me to be really careful around her and not give her any cause to think that I was a bad influence. But Mum had interrupted her and said that I should never let anyone make me feel like I wasn't worth talking to or being around.

I guessed Bharti's auntie was like one of Aunt Grace's friends, Auntie Yaa, who believed that Ghanaian girls should only date Ghanaian boys. Auntie Yaa would come round and question Afua, Tanisha and me about who we were going out with. Afua caught on quickly and would say any male Ghanaian name she could think of, but I was always a bit slow at that, so it was obvious that I was lying. Tanisha would purposely choose male names from across the world, just to wind her up. Mum would defend us and say, as long as we were happy, she didn't mind who we went out with. Then she qualified it and said that she didn't want any criminals or drug addicts.

'So don't tell them,' I said. 'Actually, scratch that. Do you remember what happened with Nelson?'

When I first started going out with Nelson, I'd hidden it from my parents. This had meant lying every time I went out with him. Eventually, I'd got caught out big time, when he'd shown up at my house with my scarf. It had been pretty ugly. Mum and Dad had been shocked that I had a boyfriend and had lied about it, and he had been hurt that I hadn't told them about him!

'Ohmigod! What's happening with you and Nelson?' Bharti asked, suddenly stopping.

'We've split up for good,' I said coolly.

'Oh Makeeda, I'm really sorry,' she said and she hugged me.

'I should've been there for you. Was it really awful?'

'Yeah, and it would've been easier if I had my best friend to talk to . . .' I added.

'Yeah, fair enough. I've been a shoddy mate. I get it. You can ease up on the guilt trip,' Bharti said.

I grinned at her. I was more interested in what I'd missed than being angry with her.

'Tell your parents about Rafi, Bharti, now!' I said.

'I can't! I don't know what to do – he makes me so happy. He's into the same books as me and . . .'

'What that freaky horror stuff?'

'Yeah.'

'Oh God, marry him then!' I said, and we both laughed hysterically.

Bharti loved to read and despite our exams she'd still managed to feed her addiction to the latest five-hundred-page horror book. Personally, I couldn't see the appeal of reading something that was guaranteed to freak you out every ten pages.

'So how did you two get together?' I asked.

Bharti grinned. 'He was in my revision class, by mistake.'

'Huh?'

'There had been a mix-up and he thought he was meant to start the same day as me, but he was a week early.'

'Hmm . . .' I didn't want to tell her Rafi sounded kind of dumb.

'I know what you're thinking, but it was an honest mistake. He even showed me his enrolment form.'

'I never said a word!' I said smirking.

'He sat next to me in class.' Bharti smiled.

'Did he ask you out straight away?'

'No, don't be daft! That would be totally illogical!' Bharti said. 'I didn't like him then.'

'A-ha, the old love-hate vibe!' I smiled.

'No, just hate! He was so obnoxious – it was like he thought he was the brightest kid in the room or something! Every two minutes he was answering the questions and not giving anyone else a look in.'

'Oh, so how did you go from that to a couple?' I was confused.

'Well, one day we had an argument . . .'

'About what?' I prompted.

'Um . . .' Bharti looked away. 'I can't remember.'

'Huh? How can you forget your first argument? That's totally illogical, Bharti!'

I watched as a sheepish look crossed her face.

'What are you hiding?' I added.

'Nothing.'

'Bharti! Ohmigod, just tell me!' I said.

'Yeah, but if I do, you'll think he's a geek!'

'Well, I already know he is; he answers all the questions in class! Only geeks do that, but then some geeks are really cute . . .' I said thinking of Nick.

'OK, we were arguing over the use of ASBOs as a deterrent for young people. I was against and he was pro. It was a class debate.'

'Okayeee . . .' I said. I suddenly thought that it was something I could imagine Nick doing with Sanari, but not with a girl like me. I've never felt comfortable in a debate – I always seemed to get angry quickly and lose it.

'Thing is,' Bharti continued, 'our debate went beyond the classroom and we started arguing in the TV room. He accused me of being a soft socialist, so I called him a right-wing idiot! Then I left the room.'

'Whoa, dramarama!' I said, surprised.

'Seriously, Makeeda, I was furious! Um . . . but I wanted to kiss him too,' Bharti whispered.

'Yup.' I grinned.

She looked embarrassed.

'It was totally illogical, right?'

'Anyway, even though I made the debate personal when I didn't need to, he chased me out of the room and asked me out.'

Bharti's eyes lit up then. It was like she was suddenly glowing.

'That's so cool!' I said, hugging her.

By the time we had reached her front door, I knew more about their first date and had already given her the details about Nelson and Nick. She asked me if I had a thing about boys with the initial N, something I'd barely noticed because Nelson and Nick are so different. When Bharti told me she knew before I did that Nick was always going to be the right person for me, I was stunned. I had only worked it out properly after seeing Nick with Sanari. I wondered how everyone else could see something that I was not even aware of feeling.

A bit later, Bharti and I were messing about with her brother's Wii when Nana-Sunita walked in. She said hello to me in a curt manner, then marched Bharti downstairs.

Within minutes an almighty argument erupted, then the front door opened and Bharti's mum walked in, then another argument roared through the house. I decided to leave. I made it to the front door, just as Bharti's brother Tejas was entering.

'What's going on?' he asked.

I shrugged. 'Just tell her to call me later.'

'Sure, Makeeda,' Tejas replied as he joined his family in the living room.

As I was walking away, I heard Nana-Sunita call Bharti a name in Gujarati that definitely wasn't a term of endearment. I realised Bharti's worst fears had come true – her family had clearly found out about Rafi and there was nothing I nor anyone else could now do. I wished I could've gone into that room and made them all realise that my best friend must have been really frightened to keep him a secret for so long. I knew what happened, I'd been there. It's like the lies build up and become toxic, and then you end up believing that the truth will make everything worse. That's the biggest lie of all.

When I'd been lying to my parents about Nelson, I had actually felt relieved when everything came out. I mean, I didn't tell Mum everything going on in my life now, but I wouldn't lie about how I was feeling, either.

As I stepped on to the bus, I could see Bharti's Aunt Gayatri making her way towards their home. She was almost skipping along the road and I knew Bharti's evening was about to get a whole lot worse.

Chapter 8

Losing Enemies and Winning Hearts

Bharti had been grounded. I couldn't believe I was being deprived of my best friend just before I went on holiday.

Bharti: *This is a total nightmare! I'm on lockdown; I swear prisoners get more freedom than I have!*

Me: *I know. I was looking fwd 2 us hanging out in London and stuff.*

Bharti: *Yeah, I'm soz, I really wanted 2 hang out b4 U left 4 Ghana. I can't believe my grandma! The woman is being ridiculous! She won't talk 2 me + keeps telling my mum it's all her fault.*

Me: Does your Aunt Gayatri agree?
Bharti: Oh yeah, you can imagine the stuff she's saying!

I could, too. Exaggerated horror stories weren't just the stuff Bharti read but also her aunt's way of getting what she wanted. She had once convinced Bharti's nana to stop using her favourite shop in Wembley Central because it was too close to a rough secondary school. Her evidence: a former student had been arrested for theft. Turns out she'd got the wrong school, but it worked.

Bharti: She started off by saying that I was just being taken advantage of because of my religion. Then she said I was being led on because he was my first boyfriend and that I shouldn't trust teenage boys.
Me: Wow, maybe in her world, but not always in ours.
Bharti: Exactly! It was like she didn't give me credit for being able 2 suss out a creepo when I met one, or actually being attractive enough to get a decent boyf.
Me: Totally illogical! Bharti, it isn't about looks.
Bharti: I know, I know, you can have an attractive personality like me! :)
Me: · Or just a huge ego! What does your mum think?
Bharti: She wants me to dump him, so we can get back to normal. Tejas wants me to keep seeing him or lie about it, so Auntie G won't start hassling him! Dad just wants 2 be happy and eat his mum's food without the threat of being poisoned!

Me: No pressure then.

Bharti: Nah, none at all.

Me: LOL! Wait, so how come you're grounded?

Bharti: I lied to them about where I was for months. That's
        what really upset them.

Me: Yeah, mine were like that about Nelson.

Bharti: Yeah, but they never gave you an ultimatum. My nan
        is like, dump him immediately or I'll never speak 2 u
        again. My parents want me 2 make up my mind
        pronto, but either way I'm still grounded 4 lying. I
        wish I knew what to do! I wish they'd never found
        out. I actually wanted 2 enjoy the summer hols. I
        must be the only kid in London who's just begun
        their summer hols being grounded! You know what?
        I had more flipping freedom when I was in revision
        mode! This is totally illogical! What you doing?

Me: Got my jabs done and been shopping 4 hol. About to
        go to Nick's.

Bharti: Have fun!

Me: OK, chat soon. X

I really felt sorry for Bharti; it was hard enough being
grounded without all the extra grief from her nana and aunt. I
hurried out to Nick's, as I knew it would be the last time we
saw each other for a while. I was leaving for Ghana within a
week and Mum would need my help with the packing closer
to the time we left. So I suggested I'd drop round with his
books and he said I could watch a DVD with him and have

dinner. Mum, Dad and Delphy were all out, so the thought of having dinner somewhere other than home was very appealing. This wasn't the first time I'd seen him since our almost-kiss, but it would be the first time we'd seen each other since Nelson and I had split up. I told Nick a few days after I'd split up with Nelson. He just went quiet on the phone and asked if I was OK. It still felt raw so I changed the subject. I knew I'd made the right decision but I wasn't ready to discuss it then.

I was still a bit nervous deciding about the puberty ceremony, but that was nothing compared to the butterflies in my stomach on the way to Nick's. I felt sick and, worse of all, I was nervous. I hated feeling nervous. Things always went awry. I felt better when I had something else to concentrate on – that was why talking to Bharti on IM had helped. Now all I could do was the bus-stop countdown to Nick's stop.

I had just jumped off the bus, when I saw a girl heading towards me.

As she approached, I could see clearly that she was one of *those* girls. The girls who never ever cut themselves shaving their legs, or smudge their eye make-up in a non-rock-star way. She looked immaculate in her lilac hijab, indigo jeans, white shirt and lilac flats. The girl's make-up was just like something out of one of my mum's magazines. It was Sanari.

'Hey, Makeeda!' she said, smiling at me.

'Oh hi, Sanari,' I replied brightly, trying not to completely freak out.

Please, please, please, let her tell me that she hadn't just come from Nick's house and had actually been to the library or something, even though she has no books and a tiny handbag.

'Nick told me you were on your way, so I thought I'd better leave you to it.'

'Huh? You were with Nick?'

'Yeah,' Sanari said. 'He was helping me out with a job application.'

Oh great! So that meant they'd been sitting really close together at a table in Nick's house. She *was* with Nick! That was it! GAME OVER! I was officially the loser in *Quest for Nick's Heart*. It was like I reached level ten, then found out there was another hidden level that I didn't have the passwords for.

'You OK, Makeeda?'

'Um . . . yeah,' I lied.

'Listen, I'd better go or I'll miss my bus. You look really nice by the way.' Sanari smiled.

'Um . . . thanks,' I replied. *It's kind of wasted now he's your boyfriend*, I thought.

'See you around!' she said.

That was it. Sanari left and took all my hopes of a relationship with Nick with her on the H12 bus. I was actually frozen to the spot. I only realised I hadn't moved when she waved at me from her seat. She probably thought I was being polite by waiting for her bus to leave!

My phone beeped.

Nick: *W R U?*
Me: *I'm in Wood Green.*
Nick: *What? That's miles away. You're meant to be here with me!*
Me: *Just kidding. B there in 10. I can't stay long tho.*
Nick: *Whatever, hurry up!*

Well, at least he still wanted to see me. I couldn't bear the thought of being around him for longer than I had to, so I had lied about needing to leave. I'd rather be alone than have him go on and on about Sanari, Miss Wonderful!

I walked up the drive to Nick's house. It was a detached house in the posh side of Pinner. His drive could fit four cars easily and his garden was the size of a small field. I'd heard Nick's mum and mine discussing the house and she said they'd got very lucky with it, as it belonged to an old friend of Nick's grandparents and they'd sold it to Nick's parents at a heavily discounted price. It looked really Gothic on the outside and totally modern on the inside. I rang the door bell.

'Come on then, dump your stuff down here,' Nick said, answering the door.

'Well, "Hello, Makeeda, how did your exams go?" would be nice, but I'll start dumping,' I moaned.

Nick closed the door and stared at me for a while.

'What?'

'Nothing,' he said, and I followed him into the other living room.

In Nick's house there were three living rooms – the posh

one, the one he shared with his brother Paul and the one that was more like a study. We were in Nick and Paul's room, which was almost as neat as the other two except it had posters and film quotes on the walls. Their mum had dissuaded them from putting up posters of glamour models in bikinis by saying that for every poster of a model under twenty-five, they had to put one up of a woman over fifty-five, so Nick and Paul had decided to put up quotes from their favourite films instead. There was an air-hockey table in the corner next to a sound system and a flat-screen TV that I knew Nick and Paul saved up for last year. There were huge comfy sofas and a small coffee table in front of the wall with the TV.

I sat down, slipped off my shoes and tucked my legs under me. I felt really tired. It had already been a long day. I suddenly yawned loudly.

'Hey, hey, hey! Don't fall asleep; I've got popcorn, water, juice and nachos.'

'You've got all that to watch a film?'

'Uh huh, I wasn't sure what you'd want,' Nick said, blushing.

'OK, have you got a glass?'

'Oh, yeah!' Nick said, smacking his forehead as he rushed to the kitchen.

This was really weird. Nick had never ever treated me this well before. I mean, he usually told me to help myself – unless his mum was around, then she made him serve me. As he placed the glass in front of me, I noticed his hand was shaking slightly. He seemed almost nervous around me.

'Are you OK?' I asked.

'Yeah, why?'

'Nothing.'

'What?'

'Nothing.'

We started watching the film. At first he was sitting in a chair that was in the corner, until I told him to sit beside me. As he did, he unfolded my legs and placed them across his lap. I was a bit surprised but too tired to say anything. He hadn't done that in ages. We used to be really comfortable like this, but it all stopped when I started going out with Nelson.

'Makeeda?'

I opened my eyes. The movie was paused at a scene I didn't recognise. I'd felt so exhausted from my vaccinations earlier that I must have dozed off.

'Oh, how long have I been asleep?'

'About an hour,' Nick said, smiling.

Oh no. You can't impress a guy whilst sleeping. In fact, as I wiped my mouth, I knew I must have been drooling! It didn't help that Nick handed me a tissue. I began moving my legs and, as I did, Nick knocked a book straight into the food and drinks on the table.

'Oh no!' he said.

'Klutz!' I said, making him laugh.

He disappeared for a few minutes as I began mopping up, and reappeared with a roll of kitchen paper. I told him about bumping into Sanari and he told me about the job she was applying for in the City. He seemed really impressed with her dynamism, but he said there was nothing wrong with taking your time about your future. I was dying to find out about them, and the only way I could think to do it was just to be blunt – a tactic that Tanisha and Bharti would be appalled to hear I'd used; but I needed to know – were they an item? A couple? Boyfriend and girlfriend for ever and ever amen?

'It must be nice having such a career focused ... girlfriend.'

Calling Sanari his girlfriend made my jaw tighten. I couldn't look at him as I said the word.

'What? I don't!' Nick said, indignantly.

'I mean Sanari.'

'Yeah, I know who you mean,' Nick said, irritated. 'You're wrong.'

'I'm wrong?'

'Yeah!' he said. 'You're so ...'

'What?'

'Nothing,' Nick said, leaning back against the chair.

'Whaaat?' I persisted.

He was staring at me like I'd put eye-shadow on my cheek.

'Forget it,' Nick said, looking away.

'Have I got something on my face?' I said, reaching for my bag.

'No.'

'Then why can't you look at me?'

'Just because ...' He stared at me.

At that moment, we were sitting on his floor opposite each other. I had a feeling things were going south rapidly. Did he just want to be friends with me? I stood up to sit on the sofa, but Nick grabbed my arm. He looked really serious.

'Would you . . .'

My phone began ringing and I could tell by the ringtone that it was either Mum, Dad or Delphy.

'You'd better get that,' Nick said, letting go. He looked upset.

I couldn't believe it. Was Nick about to ask me out at the precise moment my family had decided to call me? Had my family just sabotaged my love life?

It was Mum. She wanted to know when I'd be home. I told her I'd be late, but that I was at Nick's. She told me to come home whenever I wanted. That was weird. She almost always gave me a time to be in by. I ended the call and Nick came and sat beside me on the sofa.

'What were you going to say?' I asked.

'Listen, I know you're going to Ghana next week, and I know you've just broken up with Nelson . . . but I, um . . .' Nick began blushing. 'I want us to . . .'

'You want us to what?' I prompted.

He was beginning to annoy me. If he was interested in me, why couldn't he just ask me out? Or was there really something between him Sanari?

'Seriously, Makeeda, you might wanna try shutting up sometimes!'

'Well, when you go all weird, I have to fill in the gaps somehow!' I replied, then I was silenced by Nick cupping his hand over my mouth.

'I'm trying to ask you out, you idiot!' he said, releasing his grasp.

'Oh,' I said. I'd been dreaming about this moment, but I

still couldn't get Sanari out of my head. Was it true they weren't a couple? Would he really have taken a friend to Aunt Grace's party?

'What about Sanari?' I asked.

'Makeeda, I'm not going out with Sanari!' Nick said, exasperated.

'OK, OK,' I said. I could tell he meant it and I couldn't help grinning.

'Oh, that's just cheeky, Makeeda!' he said and we had a cushion fight. I only managed two good swipes at his shoulder and then he grabbed my cushion.

'OK, you win,' I said.

He leaned forward to kiss me, but I blocked it and placed my fingers against his lips.

'Oh, and I'm not an idiot.'

'Yeah, OK,' he said. 'Can I kiss you, before you completely kill the moment?'

'I can't believe you think I'd kill the moment! If you want to kiss me, then just . . . '

That was when he kissed me – so softly, so gently, that it felt like our lips simply brushed against each other. I tingled all over. I pulled away from him and instinctively ran my finger across my lips. It was weird. We'd barely touched, but it felt amazing. I suddenly realised my lips were dry. They needed moisture, which meant I needed lip-gloss!

'Are you OK?' Nick said, frowning.

'Yeah, I, um . . . I just need the loo,' I said, jumping up and running to the guest loo in the corridor.

When I got there, I looked in the mirror and saw my hair was a mess. It was sticking up in a crazy way, like I'd been asleep for hours and forgotten to wrap it up, like I normally do. I began finger-combing my hair. I suddenly wished I hadn't just taken out my braids; I rarely had a bad hair day when I had them in. It was just spray the braid sheen, arrange the braids and go!

As I hunted around for my lip-gloss I realised it was still in my bag, which was with Nick in the other room! My panic was interrupted by a knock at the door.

'Hey, Makeeda, are you OK?' Nick asked.

'Yeah, I'll be out in a minute,' I replied.

I quickly looked in the cupboards for anything that I could use on my lips, but I found nothing. I flushed the loo, began washing my hands and noticed the hand lotion. As I rubbed some on my hands I quickly swiped my lips. Desperate times call for desperate measures, after all. Besides, I was sure I'd read in a magazine somewhere that real ladies weren't afraid to make do with what they had, and that it was a sign of resourcefulness. It gave the example of a woman who had used Vaseline as a substitute for hair cream, but at least I hadn't gone that far. I headed back to the living room feeling more confident, but made a mental note to always take my handbag wherever I went.

Nick and I didn't kiss again straight away; we finished watching the film (he'd stopped it when I fell asleep). When we did kiss, he told me my lips felt slippery and smelled of peaches. I told him it was a new lip-gloss. This was one of those 'to the grave secrets' Tanisha had told me about. No matter what, no one must ever know I'd used lotion instead of gloss.

I still couldn't quite believe that Nick and I had just kissed, twice! There was something different about that second kiss. It wasn't as full of nerves as the first. It was still gentle and sweet, but the best moment was when I opened my eyes and saw Nick. I saw and felt something I hadn't seen or felt before. I felt incredibly special. I just hoped that he saw the same emotion reflected in my eyes.

Chapter 9

Akwaaba

I was finally in Ghana!

It wasn't my first time or anything, but it somehow felt that way. Mum, Delphy and I had already spent a week with Dad's relatives in Accra, the capital city, and we were about to travel to Kumasi to my other grandmother's, where the puberty ceremony was going to take place. We called Dad the night before we left Accra.

'So has anyone called for me?' I asked.

'You've only been there for five minutes! Didn't you tell your friends you'd be in Ghana?' Dad said.

'Yes.'

'Then why would anyone call you, Makeeda?' Dad asked.

'Oh . . . I just thought . . .'

'Hey, who's got the most mosquito bites?' he interrupted. 'Delphina!'

'Will you look after your sister, please? With her eczema she needs to be more careful,' Dad replied.

'Dad, I can do many things, but we're talking nature here and those insects seem to love me almost as much!' I said. I had tiny bites on my legs from when I wore shorts on our first day. I wouldn't do that again.

'Oh, I nearly forgot. Nick did call the day you left, just to check that you'd arrived OK.'

'Really?' I squeaked. Ohmigod! I had just squeaked at the mention of the boy's name. How sad was I? I'd had a text from him the previous day and had replied, which cost loads but it was worth the extortionate price. It would have been even better if I hadn't left my charger at home, which meant I had to turn my phone off most of the time to save power. Nick had never mentioned that he'd called Dad. How sweet was he?

'Yeeess, Makeeda, is that important?'

'Nah, it's just Nick,' I said.

'Hmm . . .' Dad responded.

My parents didn't know about Nick yet. In fact, no one did, apart from Bharti and Tanisha. Nick and I had only seen each other one more time before I had left for Ghana, when he returned my iPod with songs he'd downloaded for me.

After nearly a year of nagging, Mum and Dad finally bought me an iPod. It was meant to be an early present for my exams. Initially they told me to save up for it myself but that took too long. I mean, how would I save money when I was already budgeting for the latest clothing, jewellery and CDs? Nick said I could listen to it during long journeys across Ghana, and I told him I would need it to block out Delphina.

We only snatched a brief kiss before I left which became a hug, as Delphy almost caught us.

It was weird being away from him just as we'd started out. But a few weeks apart was probably what we needed to think about what we were doing. We were both really conscious of potentially ruining a perfectly good friendship. Plus, Nick quite sternly told me that he didn't want to be my rebound guy, which was fair, as I knew I needed time to adjust to not being Nelson's girlfriend and being Makeeda again.

'Dad, have I had any letters or packages?' Delphina said, grabbing the phone from me.

'No, Delphina, and I hope you're not up to anything,' he said sternly.

'I . . . I ordered a CD. It hadn't arrived by the time we left. I just wanted to know if it had arrived,' Delphina said quickly.

I looked at my little sister. There was something shifty in her demeanour. There was no way she'd buy something to be delivered after we'd left the country. It's something I'd do, but not Delphy. My sister was pretty organised.

'Makeeda, I'm sorry I can't be there for your ceremony,' Dad said. 'You know I'm proud of you for deciding to go ahead with it.'

It felt strange doing something so important without Dad being around, but I knew with Uncle Raj's retirement there was no way Dad could afford to leave his business.

'Yeah, it's a shame, but then you'd probably be in a bar or catching up with your cousins, anyway!'

'Cheeky!' Dad said, laughing. 'You're right, though, I would . . . ' he added wistfully.

We said our goodbyes to Dad. All that was left for us to do was to pack and say our farewells to our Accra relatives and settle down for a good night's sleep.

Kumasi, where Nana-Amma lived, was a three-hour drive away. Nana-Amma had sent her car to pick us up. When Delphy asked why we couldn't fly there, Mum told us that if we drove we'd see more of Ghana. She wasn't wrong. The Kumasi-Accra road was mainly tarmac but where it wasn't, our rear ends felt it. The road was lined with dense, dark green forest – Mum said that was why Kumasi was known as the Garden City. Occasionally we'd pass Chinese road workers, who'd often wave to us. We passed farms with fields of corn. Corn was grown everywhere, even in people's gardens. The best part was passing through the villages, where sometimes we stopped off to buy freshly fried yam chips and pepper sauce from roadside sellers. That was where I noticed that the people weren't as racially diverse as in Accra, where there were as many non-Ghanaians as Ghanaians. In Accra more people dressed in western clothing, while more ntoma was worn in the villages.

We drove up to a building with high white walls topped with barbed wire. There was a maroon gate on one of them and a blue gate on the other. People in Ghana often build their homes on a plot of land, so their neighbours' houses are much further away than they would be in London. However, Nana-Amma's plot was divided in two – the home behind the blue gates belonged to Nick's nana. His Nana-Betty grew up in the same village as Nana-Amma and they had become friends when Nick's mum and mine went to school together.

The driver beeped his horn once we reached the maroon gate. The atmosphere in the car was one of nervous excitement.

The gates opened slowly one after the other and we drove in. There was a large bungalow with a small annexe. In the distance I could see rows of corn growing and what looked like fruit trees. The car parked in front of the annexe and suddenly a young woman raced up to it.

'Auntie, auntie!' she screamed.

I watched as Mum got out of the car to be enveloped in a hug by a girl about the same age as me. Mum introduced her as Comfort, Nana-Amma's maid.

We were interrupted by Nana-Amma's voice.

'Where are my grandchildren?' she asked.

I looked up see Nana-Amma in a long yellow dress with her hair in wrapped up in a matching duku and she seemed to glide towards us.

Nervously I began walking towards her, but I was over-taken by Delphina, who jumped from the car and raced into Nana-Amma's arms. As I approached her, she hugged me tightly and I recognised the smell of her perfume from when I was little – it made me feel instinctively safe. Mum really looked like Nana-Amma – they had the same eyes and were about the same height – but Delphina and I were more like Dad's side of the family. Our cousin Tanisha was a taller version of both Nana-Amma and Mum.

We were shown to our rooms. Delphy and I were sharing – I didn't mind too much because she was better than me at handling the geckos that seemed to be everywhere. Mum said that they are everywhere, even in new buildings, which is why they are called 'the original homeowners' in Twi. All I knew was that seeing those lizards climb the bedroom walls simply freaked me out. It didn't matter that they were harmless – I hated them.

Nana-Amma's home could have been anywhere in England, except there were no carpets, just rugs on tiled floors, and there were fans on the ceiling next to the lights. The walls were all different neutral shades. When we saw the kitchen we gasped – it looked like something out of one of those TV makeover shows. The colour scheme was grey and chrome and the tiles were white with grey mosaic. Nana-Amma told us that it was built by an Italian designer.

It was just two days before the ceremony, and I wasn't any the wiser about what it involved. We were having a great time at Nana-Amma's, but a sinking feeling came over us every time we got in her car – we knew it meant heading out to see another friend or relative. It felt like she was showing us off to everybody she knew in Kumasi! If we didn't go out in the car, visitors came to us, including Mum's cousin, Auntie Leila, and her two year old daughter, Bella, who arrived that day.

Nana-Amma had already gone with Comfort, her maid, to collect Tanisha from the airport. She was coming all the way from America for my puberty ceremony. Mum could see how anxious I'd become, but mistook it for meaning I was concerned about the puberty ceremony. I was, but that wasn't the only thing whizzing around in my mind.

I couldn't tell her I was petrified of Tanisha and Mum blocking me out again. This was the big test. Tanisha hadn't been in London since Mum and I had had *that* chat. About a year ago, I had confronted Mum about the way she had excluded Delphy and me after her sister, Tanisha's mum, had died. It had lasted for years: as soon as Tanisha showed up it was like Mum forgot she had her own daughters. So this was the moment when she'd have to prove herself to me. The thing was, I wasn't so sure Mum would pass the test. She'd already been going on and on about how proud she was of Tanisha for studying law at university. Every relative we went to see asked about Tanisha and suddenly everything became a 'How wonderful is Tanisha?' moment! I realised I had to keep mentioning my puberty ceremony to remind Mum about what I was to be doing – otherwise it sometimes felt like Delphy and I weren't in the room.

Auntie Leila walked in, wearing a blue dress Mum had bought her.

'Well, what do you think?' she asked.

'It really suits you!' I told her.

'Since I had Bella, nothing is the same!' she said, patting her bottom.

'That part of you has always been that big!' Mum said, before running out of the room.

'See, Makeeda, that's why I loved your Auntie Jennifer more . . .'

'Liar! Jen was worse than me!' Mum called back from a suitable distance.

It was weird hearing Mum and Auntie Leila mess around. I wondered if Tanisha and I would ever be like that without me worrying about how much time she and Mum spent together.

Everyone has a glamorous auntie and Auntie Leila was ours. She used to model in Italy. She got spotted when she and her mum were in Rome on holiday. She met and married Uncle Paolo nearly ten years ago. He was a famous TV executive who gave it up to teach in deprived schools in remote parts of Ghana five years ago. Mum hadn't thought that Auntie Leila would be able to handle not having her hair done every two weeks, or not having a regular manicure or the odd paparazzi camera flash in her face. She had surprised everyone by sticking it out for the past five years and had even had her first child Bella, but now she was getting ready to return to Europe. Mum said, despite her looks and career, Auntie Leila was the most grounded person she'd ever known.

Bella came running into the living room. She was really cute, with Auntie Leila's face and Uncle Paolo's brown hair and freckles.

'Babbo, babbo!' she said, and she ran back to the courtyard with Delphina chasing after her. She would babble away quite easily in a mixture of Italian and Twi.

When Uncle Paolo walked in, he immediately hugged me and then Mum. He was tall and had brown hair and hazel eyes. His mum was Ghanaian and his dad was Italian, and he looked like a movie star – well, he used to, before he grew his dodgy beard. Auntie Leila kept threatening to shave it off him in his sleep.

Mum received a phone call from Nana-Amma who was still on her way to the airport, informing her that I had to be seen by the Queen Mother that same day or I would not be able to have a bragoro. Nana-Amma had forgotten to tell us earlier, so we now had less than half an hour to smarten ourselves up and head over there! The Queen Mother was head of our clan, so going to see her was a bit like meeting a minor member of the British Royal Family.

Leaving Bella and Delphy with Uncle Paolo, Auntie Leila, Mum and I set off for the Queen Mother's house. Apparently there was a rule that, if she didn't meet me, the puberty ceremony couldn't proceed. We jumped into Uncle Paolo's car and Auntie Leila drove us to the Queen Mother's home. It was a weird journey. We drove past the road that housed celebrities and even saw a half-built house in the shape of a fish. (The bottom half was a house, but the top floor was the shape of a fish.) Auntie Leila said the owners lived abroad and came from a long line of fishermen. She slowed the car down and we stared at the building. 'If you get lost, follow the fish, Makeeda,' Auntie Leila said and we all burst into laughter.

As our drive continued, I realised that some areas had street lights and others didn't. I loved seeing the palm trees line the roads. In Edgware, you could walk down the street late at night and only hear cars driving by; in Ghana it felt like there was always noise, no matter what time of day it was, but a completely different kind. The insects hummed their notes through the air at night and then the chickens took over in the morning. Nothing was ever still. Everything was moving.

We drove down several bumpy roads, and found ourselves outside a compound with deep-red gates. After beeping the horn, the door was slowly opened and we parked in a courtyard. Mum, Auntie Leila and I stared around us. I think we were all thinking the same thing: was this it? Where was the flashy stuff? There were solar lamps lighting a pathway towards the house, but absolutely nothing that told you royalty lived there. The strange thing was that it looked just like Nana-Amma's place on the outside. We were met by a man, who walked us in.

The man was tall, wore sunglasses and a smart top and trousers, which wasn't quite a uniform but looked too official to be casual. He looked like an FBI agent or something. After a brief greeting and a few questions about why we were there, he let us into the main house.

I suddenly felt anxious. What if she refused to allow the ceremony? What would I do then? Mum began straightening my blouse and fixing my hair so I knew this whole thing was making her nervous too.

As I looked around at the hallway, it seemed really normal. The walls were cream and there were plants in every corner. There was a seating area and we were asked to wait there. Within minutes, we were ushered into a living room that had a settee covered in yellow flowers and a small coffee table.

Everything was made of mahogany or some other dark wood. There were carvings in a glass cabinet in the corner. I wanted to have a proper look, but Mum held me back and muttered that we'd never live it down if I broke anything.

'I'm nearly sixteen, Mum,' I complained.

'Let her look,' Auntie Leila added.

'OK, but do *not* touch a thing,' Mum said.

I went to the cabinet and peered at the shelves of wooden carvings. One had people at some kind of ceremony; each person's ntoma had been carved in such a way that you could see the tiny patterns in the wood. There was another of a woman holding a baby. These carvings weren't like the ones I'd seen being sold near the airport – these looked older and special.

'Makeeda,' Mum called.

'Yeah?'

'Come and sit down. I think she's coming.'

I quickly turned round, but suddenly knocked into something – a small table – and sent a wooden statue flying. It was a carving of people with arms and legs entwined, and right now they were sprawled on the floor. I hadn't seen it as it wasn't in the glass cabinet with the others. Mum gave me a horrified look and held her head in her hands. She was speechless – that was the scary part. As if on autopilot, Auntie Leila jumped to my rescue and began putting the carving back in place. She finished and we sat down, just as the maid walked in with some water for us.

When she offered me a drink, Mum declined on my behalf and the maid left.

'Hey,' I protested.

'Listen, you'd only spill it and I think we've had enough drama,' Mum replied.

I looked around me. The walls were lined with pictures of previous queen mothers, but there only seemed to be four photos. Mum said that was because, in the past, people believed photographs captured their spirit, so they either looked away, or simply refused to have their photos taken.

'This place feels a bit . . .' Mum began.

'*Sumsum wɔ ha,*' Auntie Leila replied, recovering from a shiver down her spine.

'Do you really think it feels a bit spooky, Auntie?' I asked.

Nana had once told me that royal figures were meant to have mystical pagan powers and that they were worshipped prior to Islam and Christianity in Ghana.

'Makeeda, didn't anyone ever tell you about how the elderly sometimes take on supernatural qualities . . . '

I laughed. No one believed in that superstitious stuff much now.

'You laugh, you'll see,' said Auntie Leila.

'Hey, please don't go wishing anything on my daughter!' Mum said, irritated.

Mum believed it? She'd always played it down when Aunt Grace said stuff like that back home!

'Of course not,' Auntie Leila protested. 'But Makeeda needs to respect the fact that we Ghanaians have our own beliefs. I mean, the whole point of the ceremony is to request blessings from the goddess of fertility, isn't it?'

'Well put,' said an elderly but strong voice from the door.

Auntie Leila almost lost it, nearly jumping out of her seat, but Mum grabbed her arm and calmed her down. We stood up as the Queen Mother walked in to show our respect. Our eyes followed her as she slowly sat down opposite us. She was dressed in a blue and yellow ntoma designed into a long loose dress. As she sat down, her maid immediately covered her legs with a blanket. Her skin was deep ebony-brown but only slightly wrinkly, which I found surprising for someone who was in their eighties. Her hair was wrapped up in a duku and her eyes sparkled as she smiled at us.

'So, you're having your bragoro?'

'Yes, Nana,' I replied.

We are meant to call all elderly people we meet 'Nana', as a sign of respect.

'Are you excited?' asked the Queen Mother.

'Yes,' I replied.

'Good! Most western girls would be petrified!'

Mum and Auntie Leila laughed a little nervously. I suddenly wondered if there was something really terrible about the ceremony I hadn't been warned about. The Queen Mother beckoned me over and took a good look at me. Then she explained that in the past this examination involved the girl standing naked before the Queen Mother, but she had 'the eye', whatever that was, so it wasn't necessary.

I looked at Auntie Leila, who had suddenly got a smug look on her face.

'You have my permission,' the Queen Mother said in her

deep voice after a few moments. 'You are definitely still on your journey. Take your time and never forget, just when you think you know everything, there's always something new to learn. That, Makeeda, is what romance is really about: the surprises.'

Mum and Auntie Leila stared at me after that comment. It was hard avoiding their glare, but I didn't want to tell them I knew she was talking about Nick.

'I think you should wait outside,' she said to me after a pause. So I went back out into the hallway and sat down. The maid came out of the shadows to close the door for me. I smiled and thanked her, but I really wanted to hear the conversation, but it was over quite quickly.

The drive home was really strange. Mum had to remind Auntie Leila to be careful on the road, because whatever the Queen Mother had said had obviously totally freaked her out. I tried to find out what it was, but Mum told me some things weren't meant for my ears. To be honest, I was glad that the attention was away from me but Auntie Leila's erratic driving had me wondering if I'd actually make it to my puberty ceremony in one piece. After a few miles, Mum made her stop and she drove home instead.

As the gates opened on to Nana-Amma's courtyard, I saw her car. Tanisha was here. We walked in and Tanisha rushed to hug Mum. I tried hard not to stare at them for too long. Something about that hug made me feel anxious. I couldn't recall the last time Mum had held me for that long, but then I lived with her all the time, I supposed. Tanisha hugged Auntie Leila, then went back to hug Mum. Within minutes they were laughing and joking and, although everyone got caught up in greeting her, I seemed to be frozen to the doorway, watching. I felt a knot grow in my stomach. Mum's animated gestures on seeing her niece made me feel like I was a piece of furniture.

'Makeeda? *Aden, wonkyia wunna?*' Nana-Amma asked me.

I immediately went over to greet Tanisha. 'Hey,' I said, hugging her. It was weird. We were so close, the way we communicated by phone, email and IM, we were more like sisters. However, seeing Tanisha suddenly made all my insecurities come flooding back. Was I going to have to compete with her yet again for Mum's attention?

'Hey yourself! Looking forward to tomorrow?'

Everyone seemed to stop what they were doing to listen to my reply.

'It's not tomorrow, it's the day after!' Delphina interrupted.

'Oh right, but you're excited about it, right?' Tanisha asked again.

'Yes, and a bit nervous,' I said. I knew exactly what she was doing, but I wasn't going to take the bait. I wasn't going to admit to being petrified.

After twenty minutes I went to bed. The mosquitoes were fewer, but I still needed to plug in repellent. As I settled down to sleep, I couldn't help wishing I could do the same for Tanisha.

Chapter 10

Drumbeats and Heartbeats

'What's that noise?' I said to Delphy.

She was in the bed next to mine and when I looked over she sat up.

'I think that's the sound of drumming,' she said.

'Makeeda! It's started!' Nana shrieked, bursting into our room with Mum. She was more excited about the ceremony than I was.

'What's started, Nana?'

'The bragoro!'

Oh man, already? Today was the day (according to tradition) I became a woman. The fact was, I had actually got my period eleven months ago. To be honest, being the last one of my friends was a total nightmare. I mean, I didn't do that thing where I pretended I had got it or anything, but it was harsh listening to everyone else – it made me feel so immature. I was probably the only girl in the world who was wishing for PMS! As the ceremony is meant to occur as soon as you got your period, I thought the Queen Mother of our clan had made a special concession for me, but apparently loads of girls from the UK and US were returning to Ghana to have this ceremony, so I was probably not that special after all.

I glanced at my watch. It was four o'clock in the morning! Didn't they know it was just indecent to wake anyone up before seven a.m.? I attempted to bury my head under the blanket, but Mum ripped it from over me with a flourish.

'Move it, missy!' she said, shaking me.

'Someone is drumming for Makeeda?' Delphy asked incredulously.

'Yes, they're announcing to everyone that Makeeda is having her bragoro.'

'Couldn't they have done it on the radio or something?' Delphina murmured sleepily.

When we first arrived in Ghana, we kept hearing radio announcements about everything – parties, weddings and funerals. Delphy and I were a bit surprised: we kept thinking how people in England would be worried about gatecrashers if they announced their events on the radio. Mum said no one here tended to think like that, they saw it as an opportunity for people who didn't know about an event to attend.

'Delphina, before radios, we communicated with drums,' Nana-Amma said, coming into the room.

'Oh, right. I knew that,' Delphy said.

I knew she was lying and really wanted to say so, but Mum was steering me towards the bathroom. My requests to sleep for another few hours were ignored.

I was soon dressed in a white ntoma, which was draped across my body loosely, and told to sit in the courtyard.

Nana-Amma's courtyard was huge; to the left was a small annexe house where Comfort lived with her cousin, Kwadwo, the gateman. Between the two homes were three rows of plantain, avocado and fruit trees. When we were younger, she had told us that she had planted one row for each of her grandchildren Tanisha, Delphy and me. In fact, it was a mini farm, and I suspected the extra rows had more to do with the money she was making. Now and again, I could see where Delphina's entrepreneurial side might have come from – Nana-Amma had left full-time teaching for farming. Dad used to say she gave retirement a bad name.

The front gate had been propped open for passers-by to see me. The drummers had already left and I was pretending not to yawn as the dawn broke. The sky was orangey – a deeper, richer colour than the ground. What surprised me was that there were already people up and about, going past to work.

I had managed to hide my iPod in my lap and was listening to some of the songs Nick had downloaded for me. Whenever someone passed by, I waved and said, '*Maakye!*'

Good morning was the first phrase I had learned, and quite an important one, given the fact that everyone in Ghana seemed to be an early riser.

I was pretty bored, but, after half an hour, there was an almighty argument between Nana, Mum and one of Mum's aunties, Nana-Adowa. (I called all my parents' aunties and uncles 'Nana' because they were like extra grandparents.) Tanisha and Delphy came running towards me.

'What's going on?' I asked. My level of Twi meant that I could only understand the odd word and all I could get was Nana-Adowa saying, 'We don't do it like that.'

'They're talking about you,' Delphy said eagerly.

'Well, yeah, I got that from their constantly dropping my name,' I said.

Delphy's Twi was actually worse than mine. Mum was hoping this holiday might change that, but, unless Delphy got to meet the couple who ran the largest fast-food outlets in Ghana and Nigeria, she wasn't going to attempt Twi anytime soon.

'Um . . . apparently you're meant to be naked for this part!' Tanisha said smirking.

'Whaaaaaaaaaaaaaaaaaaaaaaaaaaaaaaaaaaaaaaaaaaaaaaaaaat?! You're lying! Maaaaaaaaaaaaaaaaaaaaaaaaaaaaaaaaa!' I screamed. There was no way I was doing this in my birthday suit!

Mum came out and explained that Tanisha wasn't lying and that I was supposed to be topless, but she'd negotiated with the Queen Mother that I could wear a bra or a bikini top. Apparently this was to make sure that everyone could see that I wasn't pregnant.

I was furious. I mean, a bikini top or bra? It was weird enough sitting in the courtyard with people gawping at me as they went to work. I couldn't do it half-naked!

'Go to your room – there's a bikini on the bed,' Mum added hopefully.

I looked over at Tanisha and Delphy. They were attempting to stifle their laughter.

'Oh shut up, you two!' I said. I went indoors to put on the bikini top and decided to put some shimmery body lotion on, so at least my skin would glow in the sun. I was just about to return to my courtyard seat, when Nana-Amma turned up in my room and began covering my arms, back and chest in a white paste. She told me it was white clay, to signify my purity and, within minutes, she'd covered every part of me that shimmered. It was a shame my thoughts couldn't be purified, because at that moment I wanted nothing more than to grab her hands and yank them away from me. The thing is you can't do that to your grandmother. Out of the corner of my eye, I could see Tanisha and Delphina doubled over with laughter in the corridor.

I put my ntoma back on, returned to my seat and was about to put on my ear phones, when Nana-Adowa yanked the top half of my ntoma down so everyone could see my bikini top and stomach.

'Hey!'

'Tradition is tradition. I may not approve of that bikini, but if the Queen Mother agreed to it, then it will do.'

That was the problem with having so many grandmothers.

I bet, if any of my grandfathers had been alive, they wouldn't have been too happy. Come to think of it, Dad wouldn't have been pleased about this. Now and again he got a bit weird with the length of my skirts in the summer. He sort of mumbled and Mum just rolled her eyes at him. She kept telling him she'd seen a lot worse where she worked and that was the staff, not the pupils.

'You Londoners think you can get away with anything!' Nana-Adowa said. 'Well, I hope when it is Delphina's turn, she'll stick to the rules.'

'Yes, Nana,' I replied. I wanted to tell her that Delphina wouldn't do this ceremony unless it meant automatic access to the top Ghanaian business minds. Even then with her powers of negotiation, Delphina wouldn't make it easy for them.

'You won't be needing this,' she said, yanking away my iPod. 'And you'd better give me your phone too.'

I couldn't believe it, but saying no to Nana-Adowa was like telling a fire to stop raging, so I handed over my mobile.

Handing over both my phone and my iPod was just a step too far for me. I had barely had time to adjust to my new toy and it was already being cruelly snatched from me. I loved it – I just had to work out how to get Mum and Dad to pay for my downloads, instead of having to use my pocket money. When we were in Accra, I thought I'd lost my iPod and made everyone hunt it down. I actually cried. I had the perfect selection of music on it, so to lose it so soon was devastating. The thing is, I do everything to music: study, chores and walk to the shops. Embarrassingly, it was found under my bed.

Mum was not pleased and told me to look after my 'Walkman' properly. She called it a Walkman because when she was my age, that was the name of the newest thing – a portable cassette player about the size of a brick!

I was beginning to not like Nana-Adowa; her only saving grace was that she was Auntie Leila's mum.

After a while I could hear drumming again. It got louder and louder and suddenly three men appeared, dressed in shirts made of ntoma, smart trousers and carrying huge drums around their bodies. They were beating their drums with thin drumsticks. Behind them were two women and a young girl, also dressed in ntoma, who began singing as they approached me. Within minutes, everyone – Mum, Nana-Amma, Nana-Adowa, Comfort, Auntie Leila, Tanisha and Delphina – were singing and dancing around me.

More people passed by and I was given small gifts mainly by Nana-Amma's neighbours. The music and drumming ended and I was allowed to return to the house as the next stage was about to begin.

I found Delphina and Tanisha listening in on a conversation.

'What's going on?' I asked.

'Shh!' Tanisha said and I joined their eavesdropping.

'All you have to do is carry her. It's not that far,' Auntie Leila said.

'No,' said a male voice. I realised it was my older cousin, Kofi. His mum and Auntie Leila were sisters.

'Come on,' Auntie Leila added.

'*Mese dabi.*'

'*Mepɛ wo kyɛw?*' Auntie Leila asked.

'She's huge! Not even I am man enough for that on my back!' said Kofi.

'I would have bargained by now,' Delphy said.

'Who are they talking about?' I asked.

'You!'

'What?' I said, shocked.

'Keep it down. Oh and I wouldn't interrupt – eavesdropping doesn't look good,' Tanisha said.

'Kofi, she's your little cousin. Someone from our family has to do it and you're the only male without an age-related illness!' Auntie Leila said, persuasively.

'Plus, I'm really strong and handsome . . .' Kofi added.

'Yes, of course. How much do you want?'

'I see where Delphy gets it from!' I exclaimed.

'Shh!' Delphy said.

'An iPod. Plus an iTunes card with credit in sterling.'

'What? You crook! You should be doing this for free!'

We suddenly heard movement on the other side of the door, so we all jumped back in shock.

'No wait, don't go,' Auntie Leila said, hurriedly.

'Do we have a deal, Auntie?'

'Yes, yes, Kofi. Well, at least Makeeda will be pleased.'

'Oh, I thought it was Tanisha doing her bragoro,' Kofi said.

'No, it's Makeeda!'

'*ɛnyɛ hwee.*' Kofi shrugged.

'Course it doesn't matter to you, you cheeky little . . .' Tanisha said angrily.

I pulled her back.

'Remember, eavesdropping doesn't look good.' I grinned.

'Shouldn't you be getting ready?' Comfort said, startling us.

'Um . . . yeah.'

'First, we have to shave your hair and cut your nails,' Comfort said in a mixture of Twi and English.

'My what?!' I said.

'What did you just say?' Tanisha asked, horrified.

Delphina just stared at me in disbelief. I actually saw signs of sympathy in her eyes. I silently ran my fingers through my jumbo braids. I had had them done just before we arrived in Ghana.

We heard Nana-Amma shouting for Comfort and she immediately disappeared.

For a minute or two, the only thing that could be heard was the distant hum of the fridge in the kitchen.

'Listen, it's not too late to back out of the rest of this thing,' Tanisha said.

'What? Now?' I asked. But I was sorely tempted. The thought of losing my hair was too much. It had taken ages for it to grow!

'Makeeda, this is getting out of control,' Tanisha went on. 'It's like they're sending the movement back a hundred years!'

'Movement?' I didn't know what she was talking about.

'Feminism,' Delphina said, smirking at me.

'Oh right,' I said, shooting Delphina a look. How was it possible that she could work that out before I did?

'It's archaic!' Tanisha added.

Suddenly Mum appeared, ushering Delphina into the

kitchen to help Comfort.

'What's going on?' she asked.

'She can't do this!' Tanisha said to Mum. 'It's wrong to make her go through with it!'

'Tanisha, you're not going to spoil your cousin's day. I've just about had enough of your ill-informed comments. You don't know everything about our culture!'

Mum didn't stop there. She told Tanisha to stop seeing our culture as something to be looked down on, as this was a ceremony that *celebrated* womanhood, not degraded it. Taking part was like taking your place in the history of all these women.

Afterwards we went into the kitchen and joined Auntie Leila and Delphina.

'Delphina, can you please stop peeling most of the yam? It's just the bark you have to remove, we eat the white part!' Auntie Leila said, breaking the tension and making us all laugh. It was funny seeing Delphina's square-looking slices of yam in the bowl.

Ten minutes later, Mum called me to my room.

'Mum, you can't let them shave my hair!' I protested. 'I don't mind the manicure and pedicure, but not my hair!'

'What? No one's shaving your hair. They'll just take out your braids in a symbolic gesture.'

'Oh,' I said.

Auntie Leila had just joined us and was giggling. 'Did I just hear you say manicure and pedicure?'

'Makeeda, where do you think you are – Selfridges? We haven't got time to do those,' Mum said, also starting to laugh.

I was the only one not laughing.

'You're about to go into the river,' Mum went on. 'You have your nails clipped so nothing gets caught under them.'

I just stared at them in disbelief.

'Stop looking so scared. I'm doing it for you. Now get into the bathroom,' Auntie Leila said.

Scared? That had to be an understatement.

An hour or so later, I was dressed in another robe of white ntoma with my face concealed in a scarf. I was being carried to the river portion of my ceremony by my cousin Kofi. It was weird having him carry me on his back, but as this wasn't the first time we'd met it wasn't too embarrassing. I just kept hoping I didn't fart or anything, because he'd warned me that he'd drop me, walk off and then tell everyone.

I was keen to get to the river – the heat was almost unbearable, but at least I still had my hair.

There wasn't always a road or pavement on the way to the river, and as the government hadn't finished building in Nana's area, Kofi and I struggled initially. We had just reached the main road when Nana-Amma's car drove past us, with Mum, Delphy, Tanisha and Nana-Amma all waving as they whizzed by. We continued a little further and I noticed the vultures circling above the abattoir ahead.

'You know, you may not look heavy, but you're definitely not light, Makeeda,' Kofi said.

'Hey!'

'Can you hop off for a bit?'

'Sure,' I said, climbing down.

'My back!' he said stretching.

'Stop moaning! At least you're going to get an iPod out of it!'

'Yeah, so?' Kofi said, smiling.

'So, I think you should just carry me without the snide remarks. You're getting paid, mate!' I said.

'Said like a true Englishwoman,' he grinned, disappearing into a nearby shop.

He soon reappeared with a drink.

'What did you mean by that?' I asked.

'By what?' he asked.

'By saying I'm a true Englishwoman.'

Kofi frowned. 'Wait, are you denying your Englishness?'

'No,' I replied, hesitating.

'Makeeda, where were you born?'

'England,' I said.

'And where do you live?' he asked.

'In London.'

'OK then.' Kofi took a gulp of his drink.

'So you don't think I'm Ghanaian?' I asked.

Kofi shrugged.

'Is that why everyone here calls me English girl?' Back in London, I sometimes felt like an outsider. I couldn't believe that here in Ghana, people still considered me different. So where did I actually belong?

'Listen,' said Kofi, giving me some of his drink, 'whether you like it or not, until you've lived here for ten years or so, no one will ever really consider you Ghanaian. It's the same for me in England.'

'No it's not,' I lied.

'Come on, the last time I was in London, I was told I'd have to lose my accent to be considered English. I mean, you speak Twi with an English accent so it's the same, isn't it?'

I knew he had a point, but it still left an oddly bitter taste in my mouth.

'You think my Twi is good then?' I asked him.

'No, I never said that! If you were that good, we wouldn't be speaking in English.'

'Oh cheers,' I said.

'I just meant it's like an English version of Twi, but I can understand you . . . most of the time.' Kofi said, laughing.

'Charming!'

'Come on, stop looking so miserable. You'll bring on some of that horrible English rain that never stops!' Kofi said, offering his back for me to climb on to again.

'Some chance,' I said, looking up at the scorching sun.

'You know if you're good, maybe I won't trip over a rock and send you into the gutter.'

I winced. There were open gutters alongside the road, with all sorts of unpleasant stuff in them. I silently did as I was told. I realised that, despite getting paid for this, Kofi had had to give up his day and had probably cut short his evening last night, to be able to carry me to my ceremony.

'It's all right. You're not really heavy; I just needed a break. Besides, I'm just glad you're not Tanisha – she probably would end up in the gutter. I mean accidentally, of course!' he said. I couldn't see his smirk but could hear it.

'Of course,' I replied, innocently.

We laughed and continued heading towards the river bank with the sun beating down on our heads.

'We're nearly there,' Kofi said, cheerfully. Despite his tone, I could hear the relief in his voice.

Ahead, I could see dense forest just behind a row of small shop buildings. By the trees in front of a river stood most of the female members of our family. In the distance, some other people were watching too.

Kofi's mum looked on proudly, as he gently crouched so I could step off his back. Nana-Adowa called for me. She was standing in the middle of the river. Mum had already explained this part of the ceremony to me. Nana-Adowa was going to splash the water in my face. Mum had told me not to put on any make-up, as she didn't want my panda eyes ruining her photographs.

I watched as Nana-Adowa washed her arms and began a speech. Mum couldn't translate what Nana-Adowa was saying at this stage because some of the words she heard were an ancient form of Twi which not many people knew. I realised it was another method of maintaining the secrecy of the ceremony.

The water lapped across my feet as I waded towards Nana-Adowa. I felt her vice-like grip on my arms and the water suddenly felt less cold. I looked back at Mum, Delphy and Tanisha and smiled, just before I was bent double and literally thrown into the water.

I panicked. Ohmigod, the woman is trying to drown me! Is this what Mum meant by splashing my face?

I emerged, spluttering and trying to catch my breath. It was not exactly the most dignified moment of my life. I tried to give Nana-Adowa my best cold, hard glare, but the water was stinging my eyes. Besides, I reckoned she could outstare anyone.

Mum came rushing over, helped me back to the shore and began drying me off.

'You did really well,' she said, proudly.

'I nearly drowned!' I muttered.

'Yeah, Makeeda, I've caught the shocked look on your face perfectly!' Delphina giggled, as she showed everyone the camera image of me with my arms flailing around like a distressed animal. 'It's such a classic. I wish I had the camcorder with me.

'Shut up, Delphy!' Tanisha and I chorused.

'Jinx!' we said and began the little-finger lock.

'Ohmigod, how old are you two?' said Delphy. 'I stopped calling jinx over seven years ago!' Mum took her off to talk to Nana-Amma and Kofi.

'Sorry about earlier,' Tanisha said.

'It's all right,' I said and we smiled at each other.

I wasn't sure she'd ever understand why I had decided to go ahead with the ceremony – it was confusing enough to me, but I just felt strongly that I wanted – and needed – to do it. I vaguely knew that I wanted a connection with my

Ghanaian heritage that went beyond the words on a page of a text book. I also knew that didn't make sense to everyone around me – but sometimes you don't have to completely understand or even like the stuff someone you love does. You just have to let them know that you're there anyway. I realised that Tanisha didn't have to fly to Ghana for this, but she did. It made me think about my relationship with Bharti. I had never completely understood why she kept her relationship with Rafi secret, but she knew I supported her. I wished she'd been here to see this.

We headed back to Nana-Amma's place and, as I was in the same car as Kofi, I had to hear about his heroics in taming the wild lion that had escaped from the local zoo and tried to attack me, so I was able to attend my ceremony. He had everyone in fits of laughter. I was beginning to like my cousin more and more.

Once we arrived, I was the centre of attention again. This time, I sat on the stool in a middle of Nana's living room. I had Bella sitting at my feet along with a male cousin about her age, called James; apparently they were meant to symbolise fertility – not something I wanted to think about, but I kept quiet. Nana-Adowa approached and fed me a whole boiled egg, which I had to eat slowly. Then I was fed some eto (a dish of seasoned mashed yam and onions), before Bella and James were invited to eat from the same bowl. By now, some of the children from Nana-Amma's neighbourhood had joined us. Once I and Bella and James had eaten, all hell broke loose as traditionally all the other children were meant to finish the eto, so what felt like millions of hands dived into the bowl at once. Horrified, Bella screamed a rude word in Italian, and Auntie Leila almost hurled her into the bedroom. Luckily all the nanas were in the other room by then.

'So, Makeeda, almost done now. How do you feel?' Mum asked.

That was one question I was still wasn't sure how to answer. I'd nearly completed the ceremony and all I could think was . . . it was OK. I didn't suddenly have access to lots of superior Ghanaian cultural knowledge and I didn't feel that different, so it was kind of . . . OK.

The next three days were the strangest I'd ever experienced. It was the last part of the bragoro and I did nothing. I was *allowed* to do absolutely nothing! Every time I went to do something, someone else got there first. It took Delphy and Tanisha a good few harsh looks from Nana-Adowa and Nana-Amma before they realised that they had to be at my beck and call, too.

Naturally, I milked it. I mean, I deserved it after going through the ceremony and those months of revision and exam stress! I even had Mum actually putting body lotion on me, and it wasn't the stuff that came out of a bottle, but shea butter in its most natural state that glided across my skin and made it really soft.

For those three days, Nana-Amma's home became an all-female enclave. We ate and drank, and I listened to the words spoken by Nana-Adowa and Nana-Amma as they explained the secrets of womanhood. I had to turn away at some parts as Tanisha gave me looks of complete horror, and sometimes Mum and Auntie Leila could be heard coughing out some of their own laughter at the embarrassing comments their mothers made. I knew that I probably wasn't going to need most of this stuff back in England for ages, so I wasn't too bothered.

I was still being fed the most gorgeous food – so gorgeous that, even when I realised that my clothing was becoming a bit tight, I didn't mind too much. Nana-Amma and Nana-Adowa told me that the extra weight was on purpose, to help me find a husband. I could see Tanisha and Delphy nodding their heads in a sarcastic way, just out of the nanas' sight. I wondered what Nick would say when I turned up in London with my extra curves.

My skin was glowing from all the fresh fruit and shea butter, and even my hair was growing from the conditioning treatments I was being given. I barely had time to miss listening to my iPod or check for texts on my phone.

The last night came and I was dressed in special Kente Adwinisa – gold-coloured Kente with many different patterns and colours. Then I received presents from Nana-Adowa and Nana-Amma in the form of gold bangles and necklaces. Tanisha gave me her lip-gloss, which I'd been eyeing since I saw her use it, but she said mysteriously that my real present would be in England soon.

The next day I had to go to everyone's homes to thank them for all the help and presents I'd been given throughout the ceremony. It was great to finally be out of Nana-Amma's house, but I was aware that all I was doing was entering someone else's to say thank you and not really getting into the fresh air. After the tenth '*medaase*', I was ready to head home.

When we got there, Comfort gave me a present from Nick's nana next door. She had called by while I was out. It was a beautiful necklace with a turquoise pendant. It was so stunning. I hadn't seen this woman since I was five or something, yet she knew just what I'd like.

'Mum, I'm just going next door to say thanks,' I said.

'Ooh, I'm coming too,' Tanisha said. 'I haven't seen Nana in such a long time.'

'Good. Don't stay too late, though, you know she's an old lady.'

Tanisha and I walked to the small gate that separated the two compounds, knocked, then waited for the watchman to open it.

The door opened and Nick stared back at us.

'All right?' he said, grinning.

I leaped into his arms and he actually swung me around. For like a minute.

'Makeeda, calm down,' Tanisha said. 'Nick, Nick, please put her down?'

'You never said you were coming!' I said. I shot Tanisha a look for making Nick put me down. I could have had a pure Hollywood moment, if it hadn't been for her.

'I know,' Nick replied. 'I just wanted to surprise you and see my nana.'

Then we both took a step away from each other. It was like we were both a bit embarrassed about the way we'd hugged. Our eyes were glued to each other. My heart was pounding so hard, I thought everyone would hear it. I could vaguely hear Tanisha, but she was just like background noise – my attention was fixed on Nick. He looked so different: his hair had gone completely, and his new shaved look made his green eyes stand out. He looked great!

Finally Tanisha broke into my thoughts.

'So you get a new hottie look, and forget to say hello? Or are your manners getting as bad as Makeeda's?'

'Sorry. Hi, Tanisha!' Nick said, hugging Tanisha.

'Hi yourself!' she said, grinning. 'Is your nana in?'

'Yeah,' Nick said, but he was still staring at me.

I was actually too excited to speak.

'Oh come on! I'm not spending the rest of my holiday with you two acting all goofy!' Tanisha said and she headed straight into the house.

Nick was here, with me, in Ghana. This was the best present ever.

Chapter 11

Dating, Kumasi-style

It had been three days since my bragoro ended, but it felt like a week; I had only spent about three hours with Nick and that included time spent with other relatives too. Today was going to be very different. He'd managed to get out of seeing every relative under the sun and promised we could actually go out on a date. As we hadn't told our parents about the shift in our relationship, we were doing so as friends and in a group, with Kofi and Tanisha. I was glad Delphy had gone to stay with Auntie Leila and Uncle Paolo, because otherwise she'd have wanted to hang out with Nick, too. I wasn't looking forward to telling her about how I felt about Nick, as she'd had a crush on him for about eight years!

'Stop pouting!' Tanisha told me as I stared out the window. 'He said he'd be here at eleven and it's not even ten-fifteen yet. Do you know what you're wearing?'

'No, can I borrow —'

'No!' she interrupted.

'Tanisha, please?'

'Listen,' Tanisha began poking my hips, 'you didn't have to eat everything they fed to you at your bragoro!'

I gasped in mock shock. 'You know it was part of the process.'

'Hmm . . . maybe you should've thought about the effect on your wardrobe!' she said, laughing.

'Yeah, just because I'm finally catching up with you,' I said admiring my increased bust and hips.

'Oh please, you'd need surgery to catch up with me!' Tanisha said and we laughed.

We finally went through her entire wardrobe (well, the tiny section she'd brought in three cases from America) to see if there was something pretty I could wear. In the end, I settled for a mustard-coloured T-shirt, a blue skirt and sandals.

While we waited for Nick and Kofi, Comfort was chatting with Tanisha and me about the houseboy a few houses away who had won a scholarship to one of Ghana's top boarding schools, but was afraid to take it because his current earnings supported his family and, without that, they'd be left with nothing. I couldn't imagine having that kind of pressure on me at the age of eleven. It wasn't unusual for children to work as maids or servants. If they were lucky, their education was paid for by their employers and, if not, they never got an education at all. In Ghana, education wasn't free like it was in England, so everyone had to pay school fees. I think that's why Mum and Dad made such a big deal when Delphy and I moaned about school. I got caught bunking a few years ago and I got more than grounded – no phone, no internet and no social life. It still makes me shudder; even Delphy was sympathetic.

When the doorbell rang, I jumped up and almost ran to the front door. I was on high Nick alert, and I was nervy.

Tanisha spilled her drink chasing after me. 'Makeeda! Makeeda!'

'Isn't opening the door my job?' Comfort asked, confused at my behaviour.

'Hey, London cousin!' Kofi was standing there with open arms and a huge smile.

'Oh, hi,' I said. I could barely conceal my disappointment.

'Come on, I brought fresh pineapples and watermelons,' he said, handing them to Comfort. 'What's wrong?'

'Nothing. She's waiting for her friend,' Tanisha replied.

We headed into the living room, where Kofi grabbed the control and changed it to CNN.

'Oh help yourself!' Tanisha said.

'This is my home too,' he said in Twi.

'*Kofi ni?*' Mum called from the garden.

'Auntie?' Kofi replied and Comfort deftly handed him a plate with the pineapple he had just brought with him, peeled and sliced. Comfort was the quickest pineapple peeler ever! All the local maids were sent to Nana-Amma's to get basic training, because Comfort was seen as the perfect maid. She was fifteen like me – I couldn't believe how different our lives were. Nana-Amma had sent her to school and tried to persuade her to go beyond Ghana's equivalent of secondary school. But she wasn't interested – she said she liked working for Nana-Amma and felt she knew enough, and she was saving up to travel around Europe.

'*Medaase*, Comfort,' Kofi said, smiling, and he took the plate out to Mum and Nana-Amma.

'Makeeda, what was that?' Tanisha asked, smirking when he'd gone.

'What?'

'Nice try. You can't keep jumping up like a love-struck puppy, every time someone comes to the door, or treat them mean just because they're not Nick!' Tanisha said.

'I wasn't that bad,' I said, avoiding eye contact.

Tanisha looked at me in disbelief. 'Maybe not on your own scale of freak out, but regular folk consider that just plain rude!'

'All right, I'll apologise. I don't need Kofi blabbing to anyone.'

'He wouldn't. Besides, I've got plenty on him from when he came to stay with me and Dad last summer.' Tanisha smiled.

'Really?' I said, interested. I couldn't imagine Kofi doing anything majorly bad.

'My lips are sealed.'

'What? Come on, Tanisha.'

'Nope. Anyway, shouldn't lover-boy be here by now?' she

said, looking at her watch.

'Yeah,' I said, breaking into a grin. I stood up, but Tanisha pushed me back down on the chair.

'You're staying in here till I come and get you. There is no way you're embarrassing the good family name by acting like a Desperate Daisy on my watch.'

'But . . .' I protested.

'Makeeda, do you want Nick to think of you as a sophisti-cated, gorgeous and intelligent woman?' Tanisha questioned.

'All of the above, please!' I said, nodding eagerly.

'Or as a Desperate Daisy, displaying a dance of romantic destruction?'

'Easy for you to say . . .' I began but was interrupted by a knock at the main door.

'Ohmigod, he's here!' I said, jumping up; but Tanisha's look alone was enough to make me crash-land my rear end on the chair. She left me in the living room, twiddling my thumbs.

I knew Tanisha was right about making sure I didn't appear too desperate, but I also knew there was no way all that Desperate Daisy stuff just randomly flew out of her head. I started scanning the room for a copy of one her magazines. You see, despite Tanisha's stuff about feminism, she couldn't live without her magazines. I was just hunting around when she caught me.

'What you doing?'

'Nothing. I, um, dropped my bangle.'

'It's on your wrist. Lover-boy's here, come on. Oh and fix your hair.'

I quickly checked myself out in the mirror. I looked curvier than I was last month, but I also had amazing skin and hair – thanks to all the natural oils used on me. My hair was in braids again; this time they were a blend of brown and red.

I walked into the garden and saw Nick seated next to Kofi and Nana-Amma.

'Hi,' I said, smiling.

He had automatically raised himself from his chair as Tanisha and I went to sit down – his manners had definitely improved since he'd been back in Ghana.

We made polite conversation with Nana-Amma and Mum, but we were all itching to leave. Nick and I could barely stop staring at each other. I wondered if he liked the new curvier me, or preferred the old version. He was smiling at me, but he was also smiling at the things Nana-Amma was telling him about the bragoro. She couldn't tell him everything, as some of the details were meant to be shrouded in mystery and for women only.

I kept gazing at his hair. Well, where his hair would've been. It was so weird to see him without his long ringlets. He looked really different – his eyes were clearer in this light and his skin seemed brighter, unless it was the sun playing tricks on me. Tanisha had to nudge me to stop staring at him, as I was being too obvious. Minutes later, she suggested we leave and I noticed Nick looked relieved. As we made our way to Kofi's car, Nick's hand brushed against mine and we instinctively smiled at each other.

We sat in the back of Kofi's car in silence as Tanisha's

ramblings about the best bars and clubs to go to floated between herself and Kofi. Our hands were almost touching in the small seat space between us. The roads were divided up by rows of palm trees, and the traffic ranged from trucks stuffed full with brightly coloured oranges, mangos and pineapples to trotros (mini vans) packed full of tourists and Ghanaians. Dad had warned Delphy and me to be careful about which trotro we chose to ride in. He suspected that some of them were around when he was living in Ghana and that was nearly twenty years ago!

We drove past a huge radio station by the University of Kumasi. We had only two near-accidents involving taxi cabs, but, to be honest, I wasn't sure why Kofi came so close to hitting them – they were easy to see, with their red and yellow body panels. We played a game of spot the tourist, as it seemed like they were the only people using their indicators.

'Kofi, can you drop us off here, please?' Nick asked.

'What by the . . .?'

'Yes,' Nick interrupted. He gave Kofi a look. 'I'll call you later.'

'Oh no, I've left my phone at my nana's,' I said, checking my bag.

'Take my phone, Makeeda. We can call you and pick you up later,' Tanisha said.

'I hope you've got a Ghanaian chip! I don't want to have to buy a phone card just to call your mobile,' Kofi said.

'Oh come on! Are you going to leave your English cousin in the middle of town with no means of communication, because you're too tight to call her?' Tanisha asked.

'Well, no . . .' Kofi said, looking sheepish. It was nice to see that Tanisha could even embarrass an older cousin in an argument.

'OK, thanks for the lift. See you later.' I followed Nick out of the car, wondering where we were going and pocketing Tanisha's mobile phone.

'Hurry up, Makeeda,' Nick said, setting off at a pace. We walked for a few minutes in the heat and against a wave of people heading to the shops for lunch; he kept me close by, holding my hand. This was a busy part of Kumasi and felt a bit like London, as not everyone was Ghanaian. I saw Chinese workers having lunch, a Japanese family going for a walk, plus the people walking in and out of the NGO building in the distance.

We walked into a huge courtyard.

'What is this place?' I asked.

'Just wait.'

I looked up and I saw the sign: *Manshiya Palace*.

'Ohmigod!' I said excitedly. I ran into the building, leaving Nick on the doorstep.

'Charming!' Nick said, following me in.

We were standing in a museum that held all the history of the Asante Kingdom. The walls were peach and the two huge rooms, one on each floor, were packed with displays and wax-work dummies of famous chiefs with placards explaining who everyone was.

Nick let me explore the museum at my own pace, which

was great. It didn't feel like I needed to be holding his hand to feel connected to him.

The windows on each floor allowed a burst of light to penetrate each room and illuminated the features of the wax-work dummies. I allowed my hand to caress the face of a woman dressed in Kente. There was no placard next her – she was nameless.

'This is just unbelievable,' I said.

'Yeah, I know. Apparently the waxworks are from London.'

'What Madame Tussauds?'

'Hmm . . .' He nodded.

Nick stepped closer to me and moved a stray braid behind my ear. It looked like he was thinking of kissing me but changed his mind. He gave me a wink and went to look at the swords to my left.

'It's a shame the Yaa-Asantewaa Museum hasn't reopened yet,' I said, following him. I'd been upset when I'd heard that the museum dedicated to her had burned down in a fire some years earlier. Yaa-Asantewaa, Queen Mother of the Ejisu, had been my topic for my Black History Month project, the previous school year. I chose her despite my history teacher's resistance, and I ended up getting an A.

'Actually, close your eyes a minute.' He had a gleam in his eye.

'What are you doing?'

'Just do it, I want to show you something.'

I closed my eyes and allowed Nick to carefully lead me upstairs.

'Open them!' he said with a flourish.

There in front of me was a waxwork dummy of a woman with deep-brown skin, holding a rifle.

'Err . . .'

'Makeeda, don't you know who it is?'

I stared blankly at him.

'Your history project!'

'No way!' I said excitedly. 'I can't believe you remembered!'

'Well, you did just drop a colossal hint, and you nearly bored me to death when you were writing it,' Nick replied with a grin.

I hit him.

'Hey, I just did something nice for you!' he said, laughing.

'Come on then, take a photograph of us!'

Nick immediately took a photograph of me standing next to Yaa-Asantewaa's dummy.

Although Nick didn't let me forget that I hadn't recognised the dummy for the rest of the afternoon, I really enjoyed myself at the museum. Finally we headed out and began walking along the courtyard. We were stopped by a man holding out what looked like a gold staff.

'Hey!' I said.

Nick stopped me and grabbed my hand. He shuffled slightly in front of me in a protective manner. We looked behind the guard and saw a man surrounded by three other men heading our way.

'Ohmigod! Is that, is that . . .?' I asked.

'Yes,' Nick said, equally shocked.

We realised we were staring at the Asantehene, King of the Asante. We stood there dumbstruck.

'Makeeda, curtsy!' Nick whispered.

'What?'

'He's nearly here – curtsy!' Nick said frantically.

I tried to curtsy and almost landed on my backside. I was bent at the waist, whilst I had my left leg behind my right, in a weird cross between a bow and a curtsy.

As soon as they passed, Nick burst into laughter.

'What was that? You looked like you were doing some weird yoga pose.'

'Shut up!' I said, swatting him.

'Yeah, pose of the child, dying for a pee!' he teased.

'Yeah, all right,' I said.

'So what do you want to do now?'

'Eat.'

'Surprise, surprise!' Nick said, poking my hip.

'You think I'm fat, don't you?'

'What? No!' he said, going red.

'I say I want to eat and you —'

'Makeeda, don't be stupid. I was messing around. You look really healthy . . .'

'What did you just say?'

'Oh,' Nick said. 'Um . . . what I meant was . . .'

'No, you just called me fat!' I interrupted. 'Ohmigod! Everyone knows what "healthy" means when you say it like that!'

'Makeeda, seriously I didn't mean it,' Nick pleaded.

'Is that why you didn't kiss me in the museum?'

'What?' Nick said, confused. 'Please tell me that you don't expect us to be kissing all the time?'

'No,' I lied. 'Once would be nice . . .'

'You're so weird sometimes,' Nick said, walking ahead of me.

'Yeah and you're shallow!' I retorted.

'Whatever!'

We walked in silence. I didn't really believe that Nick was shallow enough to stop liking the new curvier me, but I couldn't be sure either. His ex-girlfriend was Amazonian Anoushka, a model.

We headed into a small restaurant. The owner's children were busy dancing to some music on the radio while other diners enjoyed the entertainment. We sat down and ordered some Chinese food. We had had enough corn on the cob and wanted to eat something that we'd normally eat in London.

'I don't have a problem with the way you look,' Nick said, staring at me.

'Really?'

'Are you kidding? You look hot! I mean, nice . . . oh I didn't mean . . . sorry,' Nick said, blushing.

'Oh,' I said, shocked. Then I thought, *He thinks I'm hot? If he thinks I'm hot, then I must look OK, so why do I keep thinking that I don't?*

'Too weird, right? I didn't want you to freak out, so I said that other word,' Nick said.

I smiled. 'Oh. I just wasn't sure if you still liked me that way.'

'Yeah! I wouldn't be here if I didn't. I don't just want to be your friend, Makeeda.' He reached out for my hand.

At last! I had needed to hear him say it again. Yes, Nick was in Ghana, but until now I wasn't sure if it meant that he really fancied me.

'Really? I mean, you're OK with the way I look now?'

'Definitely!' he said enthusiastically. 'I prefer girls who, um . . . look like you.'

I could tell he was being hypersensitive about his choice of words.

'What about girls like Anoushka?' I asked.

'She was OK, but she looked better when she wasn't working as a model. Some of the clients weighed the girls to make sure they were skinny enough before agreeing to use them.'

'What?' I said.

'I know. I kept dropping hints that she should ditch it, but she was modelling before she met me, so I didn't have that right. Besides, she knew what she was doing.'

Anoushka used to be my maths tutor before Nick. She had once told me that she didn't find every part of her modelling career easy. This must have been what she was talking about.

'OK, so if you like me, then why . . .'

'Makeeda, we're not in London!' Nick replied. 'I can't kiss you with an audience. Besides, you have just had your bragoro . . .?'

He had a pretty good point. If people saw us kissing, they might get the wrong idea and then we'd be in a whole heap of trouble. Nana-Amma told me that, in the old days, if a young woman was found not to be pure on her bragoro, she brought shame on her family, clan and village. The offending couple were ostracised from the community and the entire village had to be purified.

'Anyway, there's a beauty in restraint,' he said, giving me an intense stare.

'OK,' I said, not quite understanding him.

'You know, it's not me with the problem with the way you look – it's you.'

He was right. I could see I'd been picking a fight with him, because of my own doubts about my new body.

By the time the food came, Nick and I were back to our usual selves. When we left to meet Tanisha and Kofi, he held my hand and we kissed twice when there was no one around. I felt more relaxed about being around him and I liked the fact that we could be completely straight with each other. It had been a weird first date, though, as we hadn't exactly been on our best behaviour, nor had we attempted to impress each other. But it felt all the better for it.

I was excited at the thought of spending more time with Nick in Ghana in the remaining few days of the holiday. But part of me couldn't wait to see him in England, where it didn't matter who saw us together.

Chapter 12

The Voiceless

'Makeeda?' Comfort poked her head into the living room. 'Do you want to come to the market with me?'

'Yes, OK,' I replied. I was already getting bored. Nick wouldn't be around until the afternoon and Tanisha, Delphina and Mum had gone to an international business fair in town after stopping off at the abattoir with a goat Nick's nana had been given as a present. This was just daily life in Ghana, but there was no way I wanted to be around animals being killed; it had been weird enough watching Comfort kill a chicken the previous week. I could still remember the smell of the feathers in hot water (apparently it made the chicken easier to pluck). Mum and Tanisha tried to tell me that it would the most organic chicken I would ever eat. I'm not a vegetarian, but seeing that poor dead bird made me reconsider.

Our taxi stopped and Comfort stepped out on to the road. It wasn't like a tarmacked road in England, rather it looked like orange clay – not soft but hard and rock-like. The proper tarmac roads had speckles of orange dust on their edges. There were as many taxis as people. Across the road I could see the gated entrance to the market.

'Stay close,' Comfort said.

Her words made me feel like a child, but I knew she was right. I could easily get lost amongst the crowd.

We entered the market and I saw rows and rows of stalls. It was huge – it looked even bigger than East Street Market in South London! The stalls were made up of tables or just huge bags of merchandise where women in straw hats were selling the most colourful, ripe fruit and vegetables I'd ever seen. It was just like in *The Wizard of Oz*, when everything goes from black and white to colour in the strange new world. On the other side, I could see people selling sandals, clothing and fried yams and pepper sauce. The smell of fried fish wafted past us, along with freshly roasted corn on the cob, making my mouth water.

'*Nsuo! Nsuo!* Ice water!' a young man screamed from behind us. He was carrying a large basket of bagged water on his head. I remembered being little and asking Nana-Amma to show me how to carry baskets and things on my head. I tried with a book, but it kept toppling off and, when it dropped on her foot, she told me there was nothing wrong with using my hands.

As we walked through the aisles, all the stallholders immediately began calling to me.

'What's going on?' I asked.

'They realise you're a tourist,' Comfort said.

'Come buy my peppers,' said a woman wearing a T-shirt and a skirt of ntoma. Her hair was wrapped in a scarf to conceal her hair rollers. It made me smile. In Ghana, everyone always takes good care of their hair.

'No, her peppers are rotten, buy my fruit instead – here's some *ankaa*!' said another. I watched as she used a huge knife to peel an orange. It looked so good.

'We don't need peppers, do we, Comfort?'

Comfort shook her head and laughed. 'No, but I think you need that orange.'

After I'd bought my orange, then two coconuts with fresh juice inside, we bought some yams, freshly made kenkey and a bag full of shallots. I loved shallots but hated peeling them.

Just as we were heading to the taxi rank, a small girl stopped us. She was about seven and was wearing an old cotton dress and sandals. I recognised the dress as the same one Delphy used to have a few years ago. Her skin looked ashy, almost like she hadn't used any cream in a while.

'*Yaa?*' Comfort said, looking anxious. It turned out that the little girl was Comfort's sister Yaa and she'd been sent to get Comfort because their twelve-year-old brother Kwasi had gone missing. Comfort was horrified and asked if we could take a taxi back to her family home and I quickly agreed.

The house wasn't what I expected. It was very modest and there were only five rooms, including the bathroom and kitchen. It didn't seem enough room for a family of five, but they managed to make do. There were no plants in the corners, nor was there a huge TV in the living room. There was just a small television and radio against one wall. It felt like a minimalist home, except the minimalism here was owing to poverty and not by design. As soon as Comfort introduced me, her family began fussing over me. She looked embarrassed when her mother welcomed me and offered their best chair for me to sit in. I declined and sat on the floor with Comfort.

I listened to her mother urgently explain what happened in Twi. It was frustrating – she was clearly really upset and I had to wait for Comfort to translate for me. Apparently, a man had come earlier that day looking for boys to work with fishermen. He had convinced Kwasi's best friend Ata to work for him and, shortly after, Kwasi had disappeared too. Their mother's main concern was the fact that neither boy could swim.

'Can't you call the police?' I asked.

The family all stared at me like I'd grown an extra head.

'It's not like England, Makeeda,' Comfort said. 'Many children go off with these men.'

I didn't know what to say.

'Sometimes people's children get swallowed up by the sea,' Comfort's mother said in English, before bursting into tears.

I couldn't really see how we could help, other than trying

to find them ourselves. We still had some money left over, so I suggested that Comfort and I took a taxi and had a look around the area. Perhaps they hadn't gone too far.

After an hour of searching the markets and asking road-side fruit sellers if they'd seen the boys, we spotted Kwasi and Ata walking on the road heading home. Kwasi was a bit taller than Ata and had his arm draped across his friend's shoulder. I could see straight away how much Kwasi looked like his mother. Within minutes we had them in the taxi and back home.

Comfort's mother screamed. '*Yeda Nyame ase!*' she kept repeating and she hugged them both. She kept thanking me, which I found a bit weird as I hadn't done much. Ata's father also ran out of his home to thank me. Comfort was concerned about the use of Nana-Amma's money on the taxi, but I told her I'd replace it out of my own money, so she'd never have to know.

I remembered Mum telling me that many children from poor backgrounds get persuaded to leaving home and work-ing in dangerous and life-threatening situations and are exploited for their labour. Usually the children go of their own volition, but others are virtually sold by their parents. I was pretty sure Ata had left believing he could help his family financially. Apparently, Kwasi had only chased after Ata to convince him that he'd be a terrible fisherman. When the man who had offered him the job heard Kwasi's made-up story of Ata's bad heart, he let them go but said he wouldn't drive them home.

Eventually, we got back to Nana-Amma's, and Comfort retold the story to Nick and her friend Maame-Sika, who worked for a family a few houses away and had come round to drop off some food.

I couldn't help staring at Comfort, and thinking about how hard her life was compared to mine.

'Why should children and young people have to work instead of going to school?' I asked.

'Makeeda, I don't think it's that simple,' said Nick.

'It should be though, shouldn't it?' I retorted. 'I mean, every person should be entitled to the same things as we have in England. Why did Ata think that working was the way forward, rather than education? He's only twelve!'

'It would be good if things changed,' Maame-Sika said.

'Yes, but how?' Comfort asked. 'This is Ghana, not England. What if we couldn't work as maids? What would happen to us then?'

'Education is so important though,' I said.

Nick frowned. 'Makeeda, do you know how expensive it is to send a child to school in Ghana?'

'Well . . . no, but if everyone employed a whole family instead of one person then . . .'

'Then that whole family would work, but there's no guarantee that they'd send their child to school!' Nick said impatiently. 'Do you know how many children who work as maids actually go to school, even when their employers offer to pay for them?'

'Well, no,' I replied, 'but I reckon that there are just as many employers who really don't care if their staff are educated, as long as they have their food on the table and their clothes cleaned on time.'

'You understand us,' Maame-Sika said quietly to me.

'Makeeda, it's just not how it is. You can't look at everything with the same London-centric —'

I interrupted him. 'Wait a minute, isn't that what *you're* doing? You're from London too!'

Nick took no notice. 'I mean, I think that most employers know that a percentage of what they pay their maids goes to look after that person's family, too. I think that, if you forced people to employ an entire family, then not many people would bother with servants at all. They'd say it was too expensive.'

'I can't believe you think like that!' I said, staring at Nick.

'You know, I'm so glad Kwasi is home,' Comfort said, trying to defuse the situation.

'He doesn't understand – how could he? He's not one of us,' said Maame-Sika.

'What?' Nick was shocked.

'Maame, what do you mean?' Comfort said, horrified.

'He's not a real Ghanaian!' Maame said.

Nick glared at her. His face had changed from being warm and open to red-cheeked and closed.

'If you were a real Ghanaian, then you'd understand,' Maame-Sika said with a shrug.

'*Maame, gyae enka saa!*' Comfort said sternly, to Maame-Sika.

'Is that what you think too?' Nick said, turning to me.

I didn't reply.

'It's a simple question, Makeeda.'

I just stared at him and Maame-Sika. Before I could say anything, he had left Nana-Amma's kitchen and was walking out the front door.

I wanted to chase after him and ask him why he'd reacted like that, but I decided to let him cool off. Before I could change my mind, Kofi joined us. He said the issue with servants, education and work was really complex. While some employers were willing to pay for the education of their servants, as Nana-Amma had with Comfort, many preferred to keep them ignorant. Kofi said it might take generations to change the way some people thought.

That evening I went next door to see Nick, but I was told that he'd left for Accra. When I asked when he'd be returning, his nana told me he'd decided to leave for Europe immediately.

He'd left without saying goodbye. I couldn't believe he'd be so angry with me. I walked back to my room in silence and sat down on my bed.

'Hey, what's up?' Tanisha asked, coming in.

'He's gone,' I said and began to cry. Once I'd started, I couldn't stop.

'Makeeda, you're scaring me. What's happened?' Tanisha asked after a few minutes.

I realised I'd just been crying, instead of telling her what had happened. When I did, her reaction shocked me.

'Ohmigod, how could you?' Tanisha exclaimed.

I sat there stunned. What happened to consoling me?

'I . . . I . . . don't know what happened,' I sobbed.

'You've just totally sabotaged your relationship!' Tanisha said angrily. 'How dumb are you? You let that girl say all that and didn't once correct her, or defend him. You can't worm your way out of this; you've really messed up and I don't think he'll ever forgive you!'

I didn't need to hear that, especially from her. Tanisha could be as subtle as a brick sometimes but, even for her, that was harsh.

'It was just an argument,' I said. 'Maame-Sika probably didn't realise what she was saying.'

'She did! And even if she's as innocent as you claim, you knew what it meant.'

'I . . .'

'Makeeda, if anyone accused you of not being Ghanaian you'd flip out. Every time someone calls you the English girl, you wince!' Tanisha added.

She was right. Whenever one of Nana-Amma's friends called me the English girl because of the way I served tea or something, it irked me. It was like I couldn't ever do enough to be seen as Ghanaian.

'When you insult someone's heritage it goes beyond a simple argument.'

'But I didn't. I didn't do that, did I?' I said.

'Oh please! He needed you to speak up for him and you didn't. That boy flew here from London, for you! Not for me, not for Delphy, not even for his nana but for *you*,

Makeeda. He couldn't handle being apart from you, so he got his injections and spent his money and you did *that* to him?'

I began sobbing again. It felt like every one of her words pierced a new hole in my heart, but I could feel my mood changing from incredible sadness to intense anger. Who did she think she was?

'Why are you looking at me like that?' Tanisha asked.

'I'm fed up listening to you go on and on!'

'The truth hurts, Makeeda, so grow up!' she replied.

That was the final straw. This was difficult enough, without having sanctimonious Tanisha all over it.

'What is your problem?' I asked.

'You! You've got everything, but you act like a spoiled brat and sabotage it. You're so self-absorbed. When was the last time you spent the day with your sister or did something for your mum?'

'I knew it!' I yelled. 'All that time I blamed Mum for ignoring me, but it was you! You're so jealous of me; you have to build a wedge between me and Mum,' I said angrily.

'Shut up, Makeeda!'

'Every time I turn around, you're hanging on my mum like a really bad scarf. Haven't you seen her peeling your arms away from her neck?' I asked.

'You're lying!' Tanisha's voice cracked.

'No, I'm not,' I said coolly. 'You can't keep trying to take my mum away from me, it's stupid! She's never going to be your mother!'

'I know that!' Tanisha spat furiously.

'Are you sure?'

I was so angry that I didn't see Tanisha's hand before it connected with my cheek in a slap. That was when everything became a blur and we lunged at each other.

Within a minute, Auntie Leila and Mum had appeared and pulled us apart. We hadn't even heard them come into the room.

The rest of the evening I spent in my room. Delphy was under strict orders not to discuss the fight, so she kept humming the theme tune to a wrestling show Dad liked watching, until I screamed 'Manhattan!'

After a while, I began to calm down and see things a bit differently. I couldn't believe how nasty I'd been. Tanisha hadn't deserved any of the things I'd said to her, and the longer I was stuck in my room thinking about her and the mess I'd made of things with Nick, the worse I felt.

I didn't sleep much that night.

Breakfast was awkward until Auntie Leila ordered Tanisha and me into the garden to sort things out. For the first time, Tanisha was made to realise that she had to be aware of my feelings, too. Then I was told that according to our custom, my mum *was* now Tanisha's mother because Auntie Jennifer had died. Auntie Leila told Tanisha that she'd always have her aunties a phone call away but that she needed to focus more on her relationship with her dad, who would never stop missing Auntie Jennifer even though he had got engaged the previous year.

Tanisha and I made up but it was an uneasy truce. We both acknowledged that we should never have fought like that, but neither of us was willing to take back any of the words we'd said. It meant that we were polite but not friendly and, despite several attempts by Mum and Auntie Leila, we boarded our flights that way. Deep down I was glad I'd finally confronted Tanisha. Even though I realised I shouldn't have been so unkind, I was glad she knew how I felt about her and Mum. For the first time, I didn't feel guilty about being jealous of their bond.

But I was also starting to understand that Tanisha might feel worried about her dad getting married again and possibly having another family. It had never crossed my mind before that she would prefer being with Mum for that reason.

I remembered what Tanisha had said about me being self-absorbed. Maybe she was right, after all. And maybe I'd messed things up with Nick for good.

Chapter 13

Home Comforts

My phone rang and Bharti's name flashed up.

'Hey, how are you? Anything?' Bharti asked.

'Nope.'

I'd been back in London for a week and I hadn't heard a word from Nick. I'd been so pleased to be home, but every five minutes my mind would drift back to him. I'd thought that he would've calmed down by now, but he hadn't returned any of my texts.

'You need to do something,' said Bharti. 'Anyway, I'm coming round. We need to sort out our outfits and accessories for Friday.'

Friday was our school prom. It was for the Year Elevens of the three local schools in the area: my school, Nelson and

Nick's school and the mixed school in Wealdstone. Normally everyone would be discussing something as huge as a prom for ages, but because of our exams we were all just really glad that the school and Year Tens were organising it on our behalf.

Within half an hour, Bharti was at my house sitting on my bed. We spent twenty minutes checking out the shops online, so we knew what we wanted to try later.

'Makeeda, you need to find out where he is,' Bharti said.

'How do I do that?' I asked.

'Go to his house or call his mum.'

'What if he's home and just ignoring me?'

'Then you're just going to have to deal with it. I mean, that was the worst moment ever to go quiet!'

'Don't get mad with me, Bharti; I know how much I've messed up,' I said.

'Good. That should make it easier to apologise to him.'

Bharti had had no sympathy for me when I'd told her what had happened in Ghana.

Bharti handed over the phone to me and I dialled the number. It rang four times before being answered. I asked for Nick, but his mother told me he was away in Poland with his brother and grandfather – some sort of family emergency. She told me to try his mobile, as she wasn't sure how long they'd be there.

So he had his mobile. He was definitely ignoring me. We were over.

'Poland?' Bharti looked concerned.

'I know, you're thinking he's probably already had a holiday romance with a gorgeous Polish girl.'

'Nooo!' Bharti lied. 'I was thinking he probably hasn't had any time to meet anyone. Especially if he's there for a family emergency.'

I shrugged.

Bharti and I were about to head out for the shops when we heard Mum scream. We ran downstairs to find her staring at a delivery for Delphy that was being piled all along the hallway.

'Where is your sister?' Mum asked.

'She's gone to see Daniel,' I said, unable to tear my eyes away from the boxes still being brought in.

'Her unofficial business partner!' Mum said angrily. 'He lives on Gordon Avenue, right?'

'Yeah, number 330. Mum, did Delphy order all of that?'

'Yes, she did, and she promised us, she *promised* us she'd stay out of trouble!' Mum grabbed her car keys and left.

'Aren't you going to text Delphy and let her know your Mum's . . .' Bharti began, but I smirked at her. 'Makeeda, don't be mean. She'd do it for you.'

'I never said a word!' I replied. The temptation to leave Delphy to face Mum unprepared was strong, but in the end I couldn't be that evil. Although I did wait twenty minutes, knowing it would take Mum thirty to get there.

Me: *Mum's coming 2 pick U up from Daniel's NOW!*
Delphy: *Y?*
Me: *She knows about the packages. They've arrived and are blocking the hallway! B afraid, sis, B V AFRAID!!*
Delphy: *Thx.*

As we headed for the tube station, Bharti suddenly stopped walking. 'Makeeda,' she said suddenly, 'I keep thinking that if you and Nick are having this much grief, then maybe Rafi and I should quit while we're ahead.'

'Just because I've ruined my love life doesn't mean yours will go the same way, Bharti.' I smiled. 'That's totally illogical!'

'You think?'

'Come on, isn't Nana-Sunita talking to you yet?' I asked.

'No, she reckons I've betrayed the memories of all the Hindus who died during Partition or something.'

'Ohmigod!' I said, trying to keep from laughing. 'Blimey, I thought *you* were dramatic!'

'I know! How can I talk to her when she says stuff like that?' Bharti said, smiling too.

'What does your cousin think?' I asked.

'Meena told me that I was an absolute idiot for dating Rafi so publically.'

'Yeah, but you didn't,' I said.

'I know! She reckons I should've stayed in his side of London. She said everyone does it, but no one ever gets caught!'

'What?'

'Yeah, and she said, if Auntie Gayatri gets weird with me, I should tell her, because she has some goss on her.'

The rest of the trip was fun – trying on clothes and jewellery. Mum had told me I didn't need to buy my outfit as she'd sort it out for me, so I just tried loads of dresses on. I waved goodbye to Bharti, I couldn't help thinking she still needed to sort things out. She'd stopped seeing Rafi, yet claimed she was OK with it, that seeing him made life too complicated. But everytime she mentioned his name, she sighed.

By the time I got home, Dad was back from work, Delphina was in her room and Mum was in a foul mood. No one had opened the boxes and Delphy wasn't talking about her latest business venture. We were both called to the living room.

'What's in the boxes, Delphina?' Mum asked.

'Stuff,' she replied, staring at Mum defiantly.

'If you look at me like that again, I'll wipe that look off your face!' Mum began angrily.

'OK, I don't think that's going to help,' Dad said, stepping between them. 'Delphina, we'd hoped you'd be mature enough to talk to us, but now we'll have to open a box. I want you to tell me what you plan to do with the contents and how you got the money to pay for them,' Dad said calmly.

Mum just glared. 'You're grounded till you're thirty, young lady,' she whispered menacingly. It made a shiver go down my spine and I was innocent for a change!

Dad returned to the living room with a handful of Ghanaian flags, T-shirts and souvenirs with the Ghanaian flag on them.

'Delphy!' Dad shouted.

'OK, OK. I bought them for the 2012 Olympics. You see, after the World Cup in Ghana there was a surplus of stuff and I thought I could sell them during the 2012 Olympics.'

The silence was deafening. Mum still had the same furious look on her face. Dad, as usual, was trying to hide the fact that he thought he had a future member of the European Federation of Black Women Business Owners in his living room.

'Where did you get the money from?' Dad asked.

'I bought the stock at a heavy discount.'

'Answer the question, Delphina,' Mum said.

'Fine, I used my savings from the dividend I got on Digiworld shares.'

Digiworld was a small company that specialised in digital solutions to stationery products and Delphy had made us all buy shares in it. It was the only such company that had managed to survive the threat of take-over and not go bust during the economic downturn. I'd made fifty pounds last year and Delphy had made two hundred pounds.

'How did you get access to that money? It's meant to be locked away . . .'

'I forged your signature on my account,' Delphina mumbled quietly.

'You what?' Mum said, jumping up. 'That's it, go to your room, now!' she screamed.

Delphy looked really ashamed as headed upstairs.

'I can't believe she'd break the law!' Dad said.

'I told you we needed to get help, this is ridiculous! She's gone too far this time,' Mum said. 'Makeeda, did you know about this?'

'No, Mum.' Why on Earth they always thought I knew what Delphy was up to was beyond me. Delphina and I never discussed her business ventures.

I felt sorry for Delphy, but I didn't understand. Why would she go this far? She'd always been disgusted when she'd read the biographies of people who'd committed fraud. Something else was going on here . . .

Dinner was whenever we felt like eating, instead of all together at the dining table as usual. It felt like Mum and Dad could barely look at Delphy, so she ate in her room, despite Mum's rule about no food in the bedrooms.

I was about to pick up my bag from the kitchen, when I overheard Mum and Dad talking.

'Would this have happened if we were living in Ghana?' Mum asked.

'I can't answer that,' Dad replied.

'We've obviously gone wrong somewhere. I mean, it's like we didn't bring her up with any Ghanaian values at all.'

'It's not about having Ghanaian values, though is it? It's about knowing right from wrong,' Dad replied.

'So you don't think we're too English or something?' I asked as I joined them in the living room.

'What?' Dad said.

'Well, when we were in Ghana, everyone called us the English girls. Yet, here it's like we're English, but people keep asking us where we come from originally,' I said.

'People used to do that to me in school here, too,' Mum said.

'They still ask me and I don't mind; I'm really proud to tell people where I come from,' added Dad.

'Makeeda,' said Mum, 'why did you decide to do the puberty ceremony?'

'I . . . I wanted to do it because it is part of my heritage.'

'Yes, but you know you don't have to do anything like that,' Mum said. 'It doesn't make you more Ghanaian.'

'Your mother and I are very proud of you and your sister, just the way you are,' added Dad. 'Misdemeanours aside . . .

'We'd love for you two to be fluent in Twi, but we know the fact that you aren't means we can still talk about you while you're in the same room.' Dad started to laugh.

'Nice,' I replied.

Mum still looked serious.

'Makeeda,' she said, 'we chose to raise you and Delphina in London for a reason. We don't expect you to be completely Ghanaian in your viewpoint. You are British Ghanaians. There is nothing wrong with being both. As I've told you before, no one should make you feel bad about who you are. You should never give anyone that much power.'

'Except you and Dad.'

'Of course! There must be some perks to being a parent! Besides, it said so in the guidebook.' Mum laughed, suddenly cheering up a little.

'What guidebook? There's a guidebook?' Dad asked. 'You never told me about a guidebook!'

I left before I witnessed another PDA.

Lying in my bed, I thought about Nick. I had no idea what it was like to belong to three cultures, like him. I wondered if when he was in Poland people called him the English boy or the Ghanaian boy. In Ghana, I overheard someone call him English boy and he flinched but never said anything. That kind of thing can make you feel that you don't belong anywhere. I suddenly understood why he had been so hurt when he thought I was agreeing that he wasn't a real Ghanaian.

I felt that every time I did something connected to my Ghanaian heritage, I fitted an extra piece of a jigsaw puzzle. After talking to Mum and Dad, I realised that I'd been really confused about not being Ghanaian enough in Kumasi or English enough in London. They'd made me realise that it didn't matter if I never discovered all the pieces to my Ghanaian heritage, because the English pieces could fit just as well. Until then, it had never crossed my mind that I could be both Ghanaian and British and have two ways of seeing and being seen by the world.

Chapter 14

The Theory of the Heart-chip

I couldn't believe it. The day of truth had arrived. Bharti and I were heading into school for our GCSE results. We decided to go in early to avoid seeing lots of people. We didn't want to be around anyone who got straight A-grades.

We were about to walk into the gym when my phone beeped with a text.

'Don't look at it, Makeeda,' Bharti said.

'What? Why?'

'If it's someone who has already got their results, they might jinx yours,' Bharti replied seriously.

'Are you feeling all right?' I asked, but Bharti had a firm

grip on my hand.

'Makeeda, I'll throw it in the bin if you look at it.'

'What? There's never any need for that kind of action,' I said, seriously frightened. I didn't think I would ever be able to look at her again if she tried to kill my mobile phone.

'Just trust me,' Bharti reiterated.

'Fine, let's get this over with,' I replied.

It's a nightmare knowing that you have a text unread in your inbox. It feels really unnatural. Messages are meant to be read, not to be left to gather technological dust. I mean, how long can anyone stare at the little envelope stuck at the top of their mobile phone without succumbing. What if it was Nick? What if Nick decided that this would be the day he'd contact me?

Mr Patel handed over the envelope containing my future, but all I could think about was the other unopened envelope on my phone. That thought only lasted for a minute, because Bharti poked me very hard in the ribs and said, 'Open it Makeeda!'

I tore open the envelope to read my results and I gasped. 'Ohmigod!'

English literature: A
English language: A
Maths: A
History: A
French: B
Sociology: B
I.T.: B

Science: BB
Media: B
R.E.: B

Bharti and I swapped our sheets. She got three more As than me and they were in science so she was pleased.

We immediately rushed outside to call our parents. Mum and Dad wanted me to come home, but I said I wanted to hang out with Bharti for a while. We began walking away from school and Bharti called Rafi to exchange exam results, allowing me to finally check my text.

Nelson: *How did u do? I got 2 As and 5 Bs and 3 Cs.*

I was surprised he'd texted me. It was the first time we'd contacted each other since that day when we'd broken up. It felt really strange. Here I was waiting for Nick to contact me, but Nelson had instead.

Me: *Well done! I got 4 As, 7 Bs incl science double award.*
Nelson: *Thx. U did well but you're a nerd anyway! ;) I got the prom gig with three other local DJs so I'll see U tomorrow. X*

He'd joked around with me and there was a kiss at the end of the message! It felt odd knowing it was just a friendly kiss that meant something less than it did before. I knew everything wasn't exactly the same between us and that there was no way he'd want to hear about Ghana or Nick, but I was pleased that we could text each other again. At least it meant there was one less boy out there who hated me.

I told Bharti that Nelson would be DJing at our prom.

'Ohmigod, that's going to be awkward,' she said.

'Thanks, I feel so much better now,' I joked. I knew she was right, but I really didn't have any space in my mind to think about it.

'Well, at least he'll be busy DJing. I mean, there'll be loads of kids at this prom, you might not even see him.' Bharti shrugged.

'Do you think?'

'No, you'll probably bump into him. Sorry, Makeeda, Sod's Law.'

I knew Bharti was right. We walked into the coffee shop and ordered our drinks. I was grateful that it wasn't as packed as usual. Most people just wanted to buy their stuff and walk around in the sun, but Bharti and I needed to talk.

'So Nick still hasn't called or anything?' Bharti asked.

I shook my head.

'Do you want me to call him?'

'No way!' I said, horrified. 'This is my mess, I'll sort it out. What's going on with you and Rafi?'

Bharti's face lit up. 'Mum said she'd had enough of this argument and made me choose. She said, as long as I was aware that Nana-Sunita would never ever accept Rafi and that I'd probably be cut from her will, then it was OK with her and Dad if I continued seeing him. They wanted to meet him first though. Makeeda, you seem shocked.'

'No, I'm really pleased for you, Bharti!' I said, but couldn't stop my mind from drifting back to Nick. 'I'm just glad one of us has a love life that's working out.'

'Well, yours will too. You can come with us to the prom,' she said kindly.

'Thanks, but I really don't want to be *that* girl,' I said.

'What girl?' Bharti asked.

'You know, that girl who goes everywhere with her best friend and her best friend's boyfriend.'

'Excuse me, what do you think I did last year with you and Nelson at the end of term party?'

'Yeah, but that was different.' I replied. 'We'd been together ages – you and Rafi haven't been going out for long.'

'Oh shut up! You're coming with us and that's that!' Bharti said defiantly. 'I'm sure Nick won't stay mad much longer,' she said, putting an arm across my shoulder. 'Hey, why don't you text him your maths result?'

'OK,' I said.

Me: *I got an A for maths, thx for all your help. Hope U R OK? X*

I stared at my mobile phone for a good ten minutes, hoping and praying that the envelope symbol would appear at the top of the screen. It didn't, so I stuffed my phone in my bag. I was beginning to hate having a mobile phone. It just seemed to symbolise my disappointment and failure.

'You seem heartbroken . . .' Bharti said in a faint whisper.

For some reason this angered me. I didn't want to be a victim in anyone's eyes!

'I am *not* heartbroken!' I said, louder than I would have liked.

'OK, OK,' Bharti said, holding her hands up. 'So you're not heartbroken.'

'I'm not a wreck like those girls who think boys are everything. I've just got a chip. It's a small chip that's fallen from my oversized heart. Nothing's broken and nothing's beyond repair.'

'Uh huh,' Bharti murmured, sipping her drink.

'I just reckon hearts should come with a guarantee or something, because sometimes they can take a lot of battering.'

'Yup,' Bharti said.

'Thing is, because they don't, we should probably take better care of them,' I went on.

Bharti nodded.

'I just wish someone had told me the truth.'

'What truth?' Bharti asked.

'The fact that, if you get too many chips, they can lead to cracks and eventually a broken heart.'

'OK, so is that what you've got?' she asked.

'No, you're not listening,' I said.

'Oh I am, and so is everyone else in this place.'

I glanced around and it looked like I had the attention of everyone in the café. People who were five, twenty and even forty years older than me were pretending badly to not be listening. An elderly woman looked me straight in the eye and said, 'Well, go on then, dear.'

'The thing is, a broken heart isn't easily mended. We'd need industrial-strength glue, or just a lot of time . . . and chocolate cake,' I said.

Bharti stared at me for some time and the silence between us seemed to be echoed throughout the café.

'Ohmigod, Makeeda. Did that come out of a magazine or something?' she said finally.

'No, but I really wish it had. Then I could pretend that it was something I'd read about and didn't really feel,' I said quietly.

Silence enveloped us again, for five long minutes. It was only broken when the sales assistant placed two slices of chocolate cake on our table.

'We didn't order this,' I said.

'No, that old lady did, and she said she hopes you don't get any more chips.'

Bharti and I looked up just in time to see the elderly lady leave.

'Thanks!' we chorused.

She smiled and waved. 'You're welcome.'

'Wow, you should go all weird on me more often, if it means we get freebies,' Bharti said, tucking into her cake.

I smiled and our conversation turned to the upcoming prom. We both had our outfits, although Mum was going to surprise me with mine tonight, as she and Tanisha had ordered it for me from America.

I got home to find my new dress. It was a dark-green sleeveless kind of fifties style, except a strip of Kente was around the waist. I even had matching shoes.

'Mum, it's beautiful!' I gasped.

'I know. You'll look fantastic. I'll call Tanisha so you can thank her,' Mum said, disappearing to get the phone.

Even though the dress was stunning, I was about to go to a prom that my ex-boyfriend was DJing at and I didn't have a date. In fact, I was probably the only girl going with her best friend and her boyfriend, instead of her own.

'Here she is,' Mum said, handing over the phone.

'So what do you think?' Tanisha asked eagerly. It was as if our row in Ghana had never happened.

'It's really lovely. Thanks,' I replied.

'I know, and you'll fill it out in all the right places now. It wouldn't have looked so good if you'd been slimmer; you haven't lost any weight or anything, have you?'

'Nah, I'm still the same me with additional curves,' I said.

'So what's up?'

I told her how I still hadn't heard from Nick.

'Have you thought about writing to him?' she asked.

'Yeah, I emailed him a while back. I just told him to contact me as soon as he got back from his trip.'

'No, I don't mean email or text messages; I mean snail mail. You know, pen and paper writing,' Tanisha said.

'What?'

'Yeah, write him a letter,' Tanisha continued. 'I know in all those magazines it tells you never to write letters to someone you like but this is different.'

'How?'

'You've known Nick all your life. Even if things don't work out, you'll still be in each other's lives because our families know each other,' Tanisha replied.

'OK, but what do I write?' I asked.

'Makeeda, write what you think he needs to hear; but write truthfully and from the heart,' Tanisha told me.

'Is that it?'

'Yeah, it's down to you. I don't know what's really in your heart! But you've got to get it right – you've only got one chance,' she said, then changed the conversation back to my prom. We discussed what type of jewellery she thought I should wear and how I should do my hair, but I was only half listening. I had a letter to write and hand deliver before the end of the night.

~~Dear Nick,~~
~~Dearest Nickolas,~~
~~Dear boyfriend,~~

Even for me, that was a bit presumptuous. And weird.

Dear Nick,

I don't know if you're still angry with me, never want to speak to me again, or just wish you'd never asked me out. I don't know, because I haven't heard from you since we were standing in Nana-Amma's kitchen, in Ghana.

I do remember the look on your face when you left. I do remember that I was the reason you had that expression and I'm sorry.

I want to explain why I was silent when I should have been at full volume. The truth is, I was so caught up in being

Ghanaian, that I forgot what it was like to be a friend. It was like I forgot how to treat other people. I didn't want to listen when you told me about a maid's situation being complex. I was wrong.

I couldn't see that I wasn't the only one who had to deal with a label I was uncomfortable with. I wish I had been braver then. I know now that I don't have to prove my identity to anyone. I can just be me and be from two different parts of the world and have two different ways of seeing it. One isn't more important than the other. I can't imagine what it's like for you, having Polish, Ghanaian and British cultures – especially when other people want to label you with just one of them.

What I do know is that I know you. You're the boy who got into a fight for me when we were in primary school, the entrepreneur who sold his smoothie recipes to cafés and shops before he was fourteen and the boy who gave up his time to teach his best friend a subject she hated.

You deserve to have people around you who can see you for who you are: amazing.

I know I've messed up and I know I don't deserve a second chance, but I hope we can be friends again. If I can gain your friendship back, I want to prove that I am the girl you've always believed me to be.

Yours sincerely,
Makeeda
X

I didn't finish writing the letter until nine-fifteen and even then

I spent fifteen minutes hunting down an envelope. I went to Nick's house and dropped it through his letterbox.

As I turned away, I hoped he'd read it and not tear it up as soon as he recognised my handwriting.

Chapter 15

The Last Dance

At last, it was prom night and I was actually looking forward to hanging out with Bharti and Rafi. I was about to start getting ready but first I was determined to confront Delphina.

'What's going on, Delphy?' I asked, walking into her room.

'What do you mean?'

'All that stuff about forging Mum's signature, to get the funds for your latest scheme?' I said.

Delphina looked away from me and returned to flicking through *Marketing Weekly* magazine.

'Delphy, I know you're lying, I just haven't had the time to ask you about it yet. I remember what you were like when you heard that the owner of punctuationmark.com was accused of fraud. You sold every product you'd bought from that website! I know you wouldn't do it, so fess up!' I said.

'OK, OK! I didn't use that money; I never forged Mum's signature. I got the money from Uncle Paolo two months ago,' she said.

'But Uncle Paolo and Auntie Leila have been out of contact for ages. We only heard from them the day we flew to Ghana . . . Oh Delphy, they called us here, but you lied about it?'

Delphy just stared at me, looking sheepish.

'Oh boy, they'll kill you,' I said.

'Yeah, but I had to. My money is all tied up in that stupid trust fund!'

A few months ago, Mum and Dad had started to put any money Delphina earned in a trust for her education. She wouldn't get a thing till she was eighteen.

'Yes, but you know how Mum and Dad feel about borrowing money. Especially from relatives!' I said.

Mum and Dad had had a falling out with one of Dad's cousin's many years ago and vowed never to lend or borrow money.

'Makeeda! Hurry up! Bharti will be here in an hour,' Mum shouted from across the landing, interrupting out conversation. She was in her and Dad's room.

'Mum, I can get ready in an hour,' I shouted back.

'Isn't that how long it takes you to get ready to go to school?' she said, appearing at the doorway to Delphy's room.

'Yeah.'

'This is your prom, Makeeda?' Mum added.

'Good point,' I said, turning to leave.

'Delphina,' Mum said in a deadly serious voice. 'I need to talk to you about your real investor, because he just called to say he hopes for a good return.'

Delphina's face dropped and I could see she was pretty frightened.

'See you, Delphy!' I said, leaving the room and rushing to the bathroom. I did feel bad about leaving her alone with Mum, but I could tell this was going to take a long time and there was no way I was going to be late tonight.

I was doing my make-up when Bharti arrived. She sat on my bed in her midnight-blue dress that made her look five years older (in a good way). Her hair was pinned away from her face with jewelled hair-slides. It just proved what I always knew – school uniforms ruin people's perception of you.

'You look so gorgeous!' I said.

'Thanks, those dance classes helped work off a few pounds! You don't scrub up too badly yourself. I can't believe you actually have a cleavage and a proper booty!'

'Ha flipping ha!' I said.

'So has Nick texted you yet?'

'No,' I said. I was trying to focus on having a good time, not thinking about Nick.

After I'd finished my make-up, Mum took some photographs of us posing like supermodels around the house. Then Rafi arrived. We'd decided to meet him at my house so he could avoid another run-in with Nana-Sunitra. It was strange seeing Rafi with Bharti; he couldn't take his eyes off her. Mum took a couple of photographs of the two of them together, and totally embarrassed me by actually crying and saying that she couldn't believe how quickly Bharti and I had grown up. At that point I was definitely ready to leave and even Dad got twitchy and hurried us into his car.

We got to the hall and had to wait a few minutes in the queue. As the number of students involved was so high, security had to be really tight: no one wanted gatecrashers ruining the night. When we got in, they put a tiny stamp on our hands so we could go in and out.

Once inside, we found three rooms – one was the chill-out room, which had mellow sounds, the next was the dance and indie room and the third was the urban room. All three rooms were decorated differently: the chill-out room had a tiny dance floor, massive cushions and two huge TVs, and pink, red and purple fabric on the walls. The indie and dance room had strobe lights and huge guitars on the walls all decked out in black and white. My favourite room was the urban room, where everything was silver, glass, or mirrored – there were chandeliers and even a disco ball. You could float between the three rooms and there was loads of space for us all.

Everyone was really amazed when they saw Bharti, because no one apart from me had been expecting her to look so stunning. It was the first time in ages that Bharti felt confident and comfortable with herself, and I think that this was partly because of her relationship with Rafi, as well as going to those dance classes.

'Ohmigod, Makeeda, is that Bharti?' Laura said excitedly.

Laura and I weren't exactly best friends and, about year

ago, it had been more like enemies. It was mainly over Mel. Mel and I had been friends since nursery and all of a sudden she started spending more time with Laura than me. It didn't help that Laura was mean to me at every opportunity. Mel and I sorted things out, but she'd barely been in touch since she'd gone to study in Manchester. After Mel left, Laura and I didn't have that much to do with each other – we weren't feuding or anything, but we only spoke to each other if we had to. She had taken different options, so our dislike of each other wasn't too much of an issue.

'Yeah,' I said, smiling broadly.

'Bharti looks so . . .'

'Great, is the word you're looking for,' I prompted.

'Nah, I was thinking OK. I mean, she kind of looks pretty . . . well almost. I wouldn't have done my hair like that.'

I rolled my eyes. Laura still had to be centre of attention 24/7 and couldn't handle any threats to her queen bee crown. I looked at her short red dress – it highlighted her long honey-coloured hair and her spray tan. She always looked immaculate. Most of us had had our nails done specially for the prom, but Laura's hands were always perfect manicured and she'd clearly got even more obsessed with her looks – I'd heard she'd spent the summer in LA.

'FYI, Mel's not coming. She's got track trials tomorrow morning or something.'

'Oh, thanks for letting me know,' I said. I was a little disappointed, but I knew Mel would probably come back to

London sooner or later.

'Is it true you dumped Nelson?' Laura asked.

I stared at her and decided not to answer.

'It's just that I heard he's going out with Ava now,' she continued.

I tried to hide my surprise. I had thought Ava and Nelson were just friends.

'You know what, we split up. Sometimes it just happens, but if you really want the details, why don't you ask him?' I said, and I left Laura standing alone. I knew for a fact that Nelson would rather die than reveal the details of our break-up.

I went towards the dance and room and bumped into Jordan.

'Hey, pretty lady! You're looking real good,' he said, kissing my hand.

'Hey yourself,' I laughed.

'You sure know how to fill a dress,' he added, so I hit him. 'Behave!' I said.

'So, I heard your best friend is a real woman. Is she looking for a real man?'

'Who are you talking about?' I asked.

'Your friend Bharti!'

'Jordan, she's got a boyfriend,' I replied. 'It's the guy who's holding her hand?'

'What already? Man, the guys here are quick! So what about you? I heard about you and Nelson,' Jordan continued. 'You got someone new?'

'Sort of,' I mumbled.

'Oh, *sort of* means you had someone but something went wrong, right?'

I was astonished. Jordan was actually being intuitive.

'How did your GCSEs go?' I said, changing the subject.

'OK, I got one A, five Bs and three Cs and a D, but D is still a pass!' he said, smiling.

'Wow!' I said, barely concealing my shock.

'Yeah, I know everyone thinks I'm a joker, but I ain't thick, Makeeda.'

'Hey!' Nelson interrupted us.

We kissed on the cheek awkwardly. It was really weird seeing him again. He didn't look any different or anything; he just seemed a bit cooler with me.

Within minutes, Ava walked up to us and put her arm around Nelson's waist. I couldn't help it, I felt a pang of jealousy. It wasn't that I wanted to be that physically close to him, but I wanted to be able to do the same to Nick and not have him recoil in anger. The conversation was stilted – we began talking about our GCSEs and the hall decoration, then Nelson left to get ready for his set.

'So you two gonna fight it out?' Jordan asked.

'Jordan!' Ava and I chorused.

'I'm just saying the ex and current girlfriend, it's kinda natural. Do you think it would help if you lost your dresses?'

'Ohmigod!' I exclaimed. I was about to hit him again, when Ava whacked him with her bag.

'Ouch! I see Nelson only dates the violent type!' he said and walked away.

Ava and I laughed. Jordan had definitely broken the ice between us.

I was surprised when Ava told me she'd asked the girls she knew at my school to vote for Bharti as prom queen. Everyone had to vote for a prom king and queen from their own school. An announcement was made for the final votes to be cast, so I quickly left Ava so I could cast mine for Bharti.

As I queued, I kept scanning the rooms for any sign of Nick. At this stage I knew there was no way he'd want to go out with me, so I really hoped he'd settle for friendship at least. I posted my vote and walked into the urban room and saw Nelson busy at the decks. He waved to me and I waved back. I could see Ava making her way towards him. It felt odd not to be that girl helping him out, but I was glad that we'd both moved on. He played an old song I liked, but instead of making me happy it just reminded me of Nick. It was a song from a film we'd gone to see together years before. I'd thought the film was a thriller, but it turned out to be a romantic comedy. Nick wasn't impressed, but we hadn't wanted to waste the tickets, so we stayed and ended up enjoying it. Every time we'd heard the song since, it reminded us of why I was now never allowed to organise cinema trips. I could feel my mood crash and burn, so I headed back to the other room to find Bharti and Rafi.

'Where did you go?' Bharti asked.

'Oh, I said hi to Nelson in the urban room,' I said.

'Really? You must be bored.'

'Where's Rafi?' I said.

'He's gone to get us some drinks.'

'Got him well trained,' I said, laughing.

'No, it was his turn!' Bharti replied, laughing as well. 'Come on, I can't even train a dog, let alone a human being!'

'Listen, I'm not feeling this. I might go home,' I said.

'Whaaaaaaaat, you are not leaving me!' Bharti said, horrified. 'You've got Rafi.'

'So, he's not you! Besides, I keep getting weird looks from the girls in our school,' Bharti said, turning to find three girls staring at us. 'See?'

'Yeah, that's because you look so good,' I replied.

'Oh, shut up!'

'I'm being serious!' I said.

'Ladies and gentlemen it's time to crown our kings and queens of tonight's prom,' Mr Patel announced.

'Ohmigod, is this going to turn into a cheesy teen film?' Bharti asked as everyone drifted together into a crowd.

'Shut up, you love watching them!' I teased.

'Bit American, isn't it?' Rafi whispered from behind us.

'Gee, where's your team spirit?' I said back.

'Bharti Mistry!' Mr Patel said, waving a piece of paper. The crowd erupted into instant applause.

'Wow, someone's got the same name as me,' Bharti said.

'So where is she? Spotlight please,' Mr Patel said.

'It's you, you fool!' I said, just as the spotlight hit Bharti and a camera transported her face across the widescreen TVs on the walls.

'No flipping way!' Bharti screamed.

'Brilliant!' I yelled.

'See, you never believe me! You're not just brainy, you're beautiful, too!' Rafi said, pushing her towards the stage.

Bharti flashed him the biggest grin and the cheering crowd parted for her to take her crown. She looked fabulous and deserved the attention. I was really proud her.

After the other kings and queens had been announced and presented with crowns and flowers, Bharti and Rafi had to lead everyone in a dance to a song of her choice. She chose an upbeat tune we both loved, and then told Rafi to sit down because she wanted to dance with me!

We danced to three songs before she let me sit down. I told her I'd decided to call a taxi to go home.

'Do you have to go?' Bharti asked.

'Yeah, I just don't feel so great,' I lied. I'd just had enough. I was missing Nick.

'OK, we'll wait for a cab with you,' Bharti said.

The three of us headed outside.

'I know you voted for me,' she said, linking arms with me.

'Yeah, but it wasn't just me, was it?! More like our whole year did, and they don't even know what a great person you are on the inside. You look fantastic and you deserve it,' I said and we hugged.

Bharti's phone rang and she went to the other side of the pavement to answer it. I found that odd, but I assumed it was because the music from the hall was flowing outside of the building.

'Blimey, if they don't turn the volume down, the police will show up!' Rafi said.

'Yeah,' I replied without thinking.

'It's been really nice meeting you, Makeeda,' Rafi said, smiling.

'You too, Rafi. Sorry, if I've been a bit . . .'

'It's all right, I understand,' Rafi interrupted. 'It hasn't exactly been straightforward for us either, so I get it if you feel weird about Nick.'

I must have looked shocked, but then I realised Bharti must have told him. I realised she must have really trusted Rafi to tell him about my problems with Nick.

'Oh sorry, I made Bharti tell me,' he explained apologetically, seeing my face.

'Don't worry about it. I'm just . . .'

'Is that your taxi?' Bharti said, returning from across the pavement.

The taxi arrived, but it wasn't empty. The door opened and Nick stepped out dressed in a suit, clutching my letter.

'Where do you think you're going?' he asked me.

I was speechless. He was right there, standing in front of me, and I'd lost my voice again.

He sent the cab away and turned to look at me.

'Well?'

'Nick! You made it!' Bharti said, hugging him. I watched in silence, as she and Rafi greeted him. Then they left the two of us alone.

Nick looked at me, smiling. 'For someone who chats as much as you do, I can't believe you've gone all quiet on me now. I got you that A in maths, you know!'

'Er . . . I did all the hard stuff – the exams and being your model student.'

'Yeah right, Ms Delusional! You owe me a dance,' he said.

For a minute or two, I just stared at him. I really couldn't believe he was here, but I still had something to say.

'What?' Nick asked.

'Nothing. I just wanted to say . . . I'm sorry about . . .' I began.

'It's all right, I know,' he said, tapping the folded-up letter he'd placed inside his jacket. 'Come on!' he grabbed my hand and led me back into the prom.

We went to the chill-out room and he laced his arms around my waist as we slow-danced. I wanted to apologise again, but he stopped me and explained that he'd lost his phone in Kumasi and was so angry with me that he decided to wait till I got back to London to talk things over. Then, when he arrived in London, he had to go straight off to Poland because his grand-dad was ill. He'd thought I didn't care about him, and couldn't believe he'd flown to Ghana to be treated like that by someone he cared for. My letter had changed all of that.

'So I should be apologising, for not contacting you,' he said.

'Seriously, how many times can you two say sorry?' Bharti was dancing close by with Rafi, and they were both smiling. 'Just get to the good bit!'

'The good bit?' I said, confused.

'Makeeda, couples argue then . . . make up?' Bharti added meaningfully.

Nick blushed, then moved us away from Bharti and Rafi.

I remembered that Nick had always avoided kissing me in public.

I rested my head against his chest, wondering if we really were a couple as Bharti had said.

'Makeeda, *mepε w'asem*,' Nick whispered.

'Ohmigod, you learned Twi?' I said, looking up.

'*Aane.*' He smiled.

'I really like you, too.' I smiled back at him.

I realised that I didn't have to hear the word 'girlfriend' to know that I was one, just as I didn't need someone else's definition of Ghanaian or British to know that I was both.

Nick whispered in my ear. 'You look really kissable tonight.'

I gazed up at him. 'What, kissable in public?'

'Always,' he said and we kissed.

Guide to Ghanaian Terms and Phrases

Ghanaian Terms

Accra
Capital city of Ghana.

adowa
A traditional dance, and also music, of the Akan people of Ghana.

Akan
Refers to the first group of settlers who came to modern day Ghana who form the largest ethnic group in Ghana. It consists of several politically independent units, such as the Asante, Akim, Akuapem and Kwahu.

ankaa
Orange (fruit).

Asante (Ashanti)
A region in Ghana. The Asante people speak Twi.

Asante Kingdom
Created between the 16th and 18th centuries and comprised of
many states united under Osei Tutu the first Asantehene. It
gained wealth through trade and conquests.

Asantehene
King of the Asante people.

bragoro
Puberty ceremony for girls.

duku
Ghanaian style head-scarf worn by women.

eto
Mashed onions, yams or plantain

Hip-Life
A type of West African music which is similar to hip-hop and
rap.

kenkey
Corn dough cooked in corn leaves.

Kente
A colourful Asante ceremonial cloth, worn at festivals, times
of thanksgiving and on special occasions. It is made of silk and
woven on a hand-loom in strips, before being sewn together to
form a larger cloth that is then made into garments.

Kumasi
Capital city of the Asante region in Ghana. Also known as the
Garden City because of its rich vegetation.

Manshiya Palace
Home to Asantehene and the Asante Museum.

ntoma
African clothing made of cotton.

plantain
Part of the banana family. Comes in two varieties: green
(unripe), which are cooked like potatoes, and yellow (ripe),
which are usually fried, roasted or boiled.

Twi
The main dialect of the Akan language in Ghana, spoken by
the Asante people.

Yaa-Asantewaa
Queen Mother of the Egweso people. She fought the British in the 1900 war.

yam
A vegetable that grows in the form of tubers. It has rough brown skin (which is peeled before cooking) and a white fleshy centre. It is cooked in a similar way to potatoes.

Ghanaian Phrases

Aane
Yes

Aden, wonkyia wunna?
Why don't you say hello to your sister/brother/cousin?

ɛnyɛ hwee
It doesn't matter

Gyae ɛnka saa!
Stop, don't say that!

Maakye
Good morning

Medaase
Thank you

Mepε w'asem
I like you

Mepε wo kyεw
Please

Mese dabi
I said no

nsuo
water

Mi papa ye Ghana ni
My father is Ghanaian

Sumsum wε ha
There is a spiritual presence here

Yeda Nyame ase
Thank God

☆

www.piccadillypress.co.uk

☆ The latest news on forthcoming books

☆ Chapter previews

☆ Author biographies

☆ Fun quizzes

☆ Reader reviews

☆ Competitions and fab prizes

☆ Book features and cool downloads

☆ And much, much more . . .

Log on and check it out!

Piccadilly Press

☆